Dedicated with love to Sister Anne Eugene Metcalf, CSJ—thanks for giving me the chance to learn as well as to teach.

(And to T.L.—thanks for that perfect day in Salem!)

The Circle Girls
Once upon a Witch

Anya Novikov

The Circle Girls: Once upon a Witch

COPYRIGHT 2013 by Anya Novikov

Contact Information: titleadmin@pelicanbookgroup.com

Scripture quotations, unless otherwise indicated are taken from the King James translation, public domain.

Cover Art by Nicola Martinez

Watershed Books, a division of Pelican Ventures, LLC
www.pelicanbookgroup.com PO Box 1738 *Aztec, NM * 87410

Watershed Books praise and splash logo is a trademark of Pelican Ventures, LLC

Publishing History
First Watershed Edition, 2013
Paperback Edition ISBN 978-1-61116-258-5
Electronic Edition ISBN 978-1-61116-257-8
Published in the United States of America

1

God will give you blood to drink.

The witch's curse still hung in the air a whole day after the executions. Even though the strange wind from the bay was hot and dry, Deliverance shivered.

From underneath the edge of her white cap, she stole a secret glance at the empty tree on Gallows Hill. Of course, she had witnessed the executions. It was a good morality lesson. The court had determined children should attend. Once again, her stomach churned. The witches now lay in hasty graves. But all night long, she had seen their twitching bodies behind her eyelids when she tried to sleep.

Judge Noyes must be shaking in his boots. One witch had cursed him. *I am no more a witch than you are a wizard...If you take my life away, God will give you blood to drink!*

Truth to tell, Goodwife Sarah Good hadn't seemed much of a witch. A slothful beggar to be sure. But the girl chewed her lip in thought. Perhaps the court had been right to condemn her. Goody Good's filth had brought the smallpox.

Well, Deliverance lived a proper life, and she had taken no part in the accusations. Relief skimmed her. *Although Ann and her other friends had.*

Her skin goosed.

What hung from the branches now? Fruits shaped like pears but deep dark green with rough bubbled skin like a frog? She rubbed her eyes and the vision disappeared.

The wind turned suddenly moist and cold. Icy fingers climbed up the ladder of her spine. Had they been witches after all? Hadn't the witch of Endor conjured the image of the prophet Samuel for King Saul, those ancient centuries past? Her stomach churned. Had not the prophet Isaiah explained that spirits and powers of the dark could peek into man's affairs?

She rubbed her eyes another time. What *was* this strange fruit with the skin of frogs hanging where five witches had met their judgment? Some corruption from the Tree of Knowledge of Good and Evil?

Everyone knew that frogs and toads were diabolical. The Book of Revelation said so. Why would she imagine such a wicked thing?

Unless she herself was bewitched.

But no. She could not be. There was no bewitchment. Her mother had explained it. Just jealousies and resentments against neighbors, suspicion against things not understood. Distrust for those who did not follow the rules. The accusations were all falsehoods.

She and her honored mother had discussed this very thing just two nights ago while they mended by firelight, in voices so soft they could hardly hear each other. After all, someone could be listening. Even though the hour was late, the night dark, and the nearest neighbor many acres away.

"Aye, my mother," Deliverance had sighed. "I do not understand the court's authority. Goodwife Nurse speaks crossly to her husband when she cannot hear him plainly. Because she is old and deaf! How does that cause doubt about her faith in Christ and brand her a witch?" At these words, she had pricked her finger and dotted a linen napkin with blood. That could not be a good sign.

Her mother had bent close with a comforting hand. "The circle girls rant against Rebecca Nurse, daughter, and the grownups believe them. I fear it all stems from a grudge over a boundary line."

"So why don't good folk speak out in her defense?" She looked pointedly at her mother.

Glaring back, her mother had not minced words. "I dare not say a word. The same fate might happen to me."

Just remembering the conversation sent new chills of horror clamping at the back of her neck. Her throat tightened in a terrible strangle. First her mother had just shrugged, mitering a hem's corner as neatly as always. As though these were ordinary times.

Then her mother had continued. "Deliverance, you heard the court's declaration along with me. If Satan can seduce the soul of such a godly woman as Goodwife Rebecca Nurse, then the weak must be even more vigilant in rooting out evil. Why, Reverend Parris preached on this phenomenon last meeting. With the millennium not long off, Satan is more mischievous than usual."

Ah. Satan. The Dark One. The Prince of the Air whose latest converts had swung so clumsily from the tree.

Shivering again in the near-dusk, Deliverance hurried toward home. Just up ahead was the pasture where the witch-sabbaths had been held. *Or so Ann Putnam had said.* As Deliverance approached, hundreds of spade-footed frogs started to croak loudly. Frogs!

Fear rose in her gullet. To have this ruckus happen just as she walked by doused her with suspicion. She turned hot with terror.

It was Reverend Parris's own pasture. His daughter and niece had been the first ones afflicted by the witches, one of whom was his own slave woman, Tituba. She had bewitched the innocent girls with fortune-telling and conjuring and charms. And she had sworn she'd seen the Tall Man...

But Tituba had been spared from the gallows. She had confessed and repented.

Cautiously, Deliverance turned her head to see if anyone noticed the noisy frogs. Any unusual gesture or thoughtless remark could be her doom. Her heart pounded. Almost as if the air had conjured her, Goodwife Putnam, Ann's arrogant mother, stepped in front of her with a frown.

Deliverance had no choice but to stop, bowing her head respectfully.

The woman's voice chided, somehow dangerous. "Why, Deliverance, 'tis nearly dusk, girl. What mischief? Why do you wander Salem Village? Surely your mother has evening chores awaiting you at home."

"Aye, Goody," she murmured modestly, hands clasped against her white smock. "I am on my way just now."

"That is good. You are wise to remain a dutiful daughter. Otherwise, disobedience and sloth could bring about your downfall." The woman's nose lifted.

Goody Putnam's words turned to ice water the blood in Deliverance's veins. The woman's condemnations against the accused witches had been especially vicious. Was she now threatening

Deliverance's mother? Or did the goodwife consider Deliverance's stroll a sign of laziness that would lead her into temptation?

"I have my honored mother's permission to stop at Goodman Crowninshield's marsh for some medicinal herbs." Deliverance lied, feeling queasy. Lies were a deep sin no matter the reason. Suddenly, she realized she had no real reason to be alone in the village and no recollection of how she had come to be here. The strange fruits bobbled in her brain. Her eyes crusted with the sands of sleep, and she scoured her lids with her fists.

And she realized the danger of her words. There were many who held that herbs were gathered not for medicines but for potions and charms and spells. "My young sister has a need for feverfew. An ague."

The explanation must have soothed Goodwife Putnam, for she shooed Deliverance away and headed for a gaggle of gossipmongers. "Off with you then. Greet Matilda for me. Remember to be of good help to her." Then her sly eyes brightened. "It must be difficult for you and your mother to maintain such a fine farm without a man."

Deliverance turned from the woman, mindful that Goodwife Putnam's words were somehow a threat. At least her daughter Ann was still Deliverance's friend.

For a little while, Deliverance had to escape the village. She couldn't help it, chores or not. An amble through the marsh wouldn't be amiss if she gathered up some useful herbs.

But she must hurry. It was getting dark. Goodman Crowninshield often let her hunt for herbs on his land. His woods might have been a pleasant place to play, but children were not allowed amusement. No toys.

Not Christmas. Since picking herbs was work, her walks through his bramble patches were permitted.

She hurried away in the fading afternoon sun. In a sudden breeze, her cap bounced off her head, baring her bright hair.

The color of hell fire. Many of the goodwives gossiped about her hair these days. Since the troubles had started, she was careful to watch her tongue and keep her hair carefully tucked away. One's faulty appearance or improper actions could bring doom. Shivering, Deliverance reached for her cap, but it flew on the brisk air like a white bird, gliding past the grasping trees on Gallows Hill.

If you take my life away, God will give you blood to drink!

In her heart of hearts, she knew that yesterday's five lost souls wouldn't be the last. Who would be next? Herself?

Deliver me from evil.

She glanced quickly behind her, but Goodwife Putnam didn't appear to pay her and her evil hair any attention. And Deliverance still had the protection of Ann Putnam's friendship. She was glad of that, for Ann's cruel accusations had helped bring about yesterday's hangings.

As well as the first one in June. A tavern owner who had worn scarlet and lace and failed to attend Meeting. Goody Bishop had recited the Scripture properly and had nursed the sick during the smallpox, but none of that had counted.

Deliverance shook her head to rid the ugliness and breathed deep. Swamp smells reached her nostrils, but she didn't mind. Her feet hardly touched the ground. Finally, she reached Absalom Crowninshield's woods.

It was dark there, and she could hide for a while. With a grateful smile, she found a handful of feverfew waiting to be picked. Her excursion would be better explained.

All of a sudden, both her footfall and her heart seemed lighter. The sweet sound of music rested on the air. She couldn't help shuddering again, however. Other than the Psalter during worship meeting, music was considered frivolous.

Deliverance didn't think so, but after all, she had hell-fire hair. Maybe she *was* evil inside. She ran straight toward the sound just as a dark figure slipped into the trees.

Without a thought, she followed—nay, she floated, not caring he might be the Dark One who lay in wait for the unwary along dim waysides.

This sweet angelic sound cannot be evil, she told herself. The musician does not mean me harm! Yet in the back of her brain, she remembered the reverend's words. *The devil is never more real than when he seems an angel of light.*

Pausing nervously, she looked through the swamp maples and the fiddlehead ferns. Maybe demons did lurk behind the tree trunks. Almost without her approval, her feet began to plod slowly forward through the gloom.

What if the Dark One himself stood ahead, waiting for her to sign his book? What if he took the shape of someone she knew so that she would trust him?

The forest around her seemed endless and soon became swamp. Twilight swirled about her in a mist she could feel. She didn't recognize this place. Maybe the Prince of the Air did live here, inviting his followers to unholy sacraments. Luring them to mountaintops to own all they could see if they followed him.

She did not know. Although she was afraid, she moved through the dank air, almost unable stop on her own feet. The clearing ahead of her was one that she did not remember in spite of all her herb-hunts in these dark woods.

Even in the dusk, the clearing was full of sunshine as if the treetops had a hole in them. The big granite boulders in the center of the halo of light were covered in moss and fern. A young man leaned up against the rocks, his profile to her. His long, white hands held to his mouth a fife of some sort.

The notes he played invited her slowly toward him. She could not take her eyes from him, yet she did not trip or stumble through the roots. Her feet did not seem to touch the ground. Her long wool skirts did not catch in the muck. He wore a dark blue shirt, black trousers, a cloak that hung back over his shoulders, and tall leather boots. One foot stood firm in the muddy layers of decaying leaves; the other was propped against a small rock. His hair, dark as midnight, swung like a cape over his shoulders and hung to his elbows.

While she approached, her heart pounded with the strangeness of the scene. He turned and stopped playing. His long hair covered the right side of his face, dividing it straight down the middle. He did not brush it away. Only his left eye showed; it watched her kindly, with gentle mystery, but he did not speak.

"Who are you?" she asked.

Still he said nothing, and she gave in to the temptation to hear the music.

"Please do not cease your playing. It is so lovely. I

8

mean not to pry." Her blood raced against the bones underneath her skin.

As he hesitated, she felt relief. He was correct to stop. She was listening to forbidden music in a time of fear and death. She was in a place she had not known to exist before this minute. All of this was either a miracle or a spell. She prayed for a miracle, for a spell would bring death.

"Good day, mistress," he said finally. His voice was low with an unfamiliar burr. The left side of his face, the side that wasn't masked by his hair, was beautiful. The half-mouth was well-shaped and rosy, the slender half of nose handsomely carved. He placed the instrument to his mouth once again and started a lilting tune. She could see that he held some sort of flute, handmade from a reed.

La-a-a. La-a. La. La. La-a. La. La. La-a. La-a-a.

Suddenly the dangerous sounds hammered into her.

"Oh, no, you must stop! It is not wise. Someone might hear. These are strange days. Goodman Crowninshield is a fine man, but there are so many others..." She thought of Goody Putnam and reached to stop him.

As he turned away, the long curtain of hair lifted like a bat stretching its wing. She saw the rest of his face, and gasped out loud.

The left side of his face was as perfect as that of the alabaster saints the reverend railed against. The gray eye watched her with much interest.

The right side was a twisted web of tortured flesh with a cold, dark hole that had once been an eye.

Was he a demon after all? Was this good and evil combined? Her breath came out in loud heaves that she could see in the air.

"Do not fear me," he told her finally.

How could she not? What if he was a spirit or a wizard? The prophet Isaiah clearly admonished against such a thing. But her left hand seemed to have a mind of its own. It reached for him. She placed it gently over what had once been a face almost as if she had done so many times before.

Then he took her hand and placed his lips at her wrist.

Her pulse jumped with life against his mouth, but she found a lump of fear in her throat as she tried to swallow.

"You can trust me," he said. "I mean no harm."

She turned from him, filled with interest but also with loathing.

"Trust?" She wanted to escape. "Trust does not exist here in Salem Village." For the first time, her feet seemed stuck in the mud.

"I will find you, you know," he told her confidently.

Startled, she looked at him one last time.

He pointed to the eyeless hole. "I am not blind. I see most everything." Then his voice sounded sad.

"But I cannot see yet if you are my doom or my deliverance. Maybe you are both. Or maybe I am yours." With no other word, he turned and swiftly vanished into the evening trees.

His deliverance? Her skin crawled, for he had spoken her name. At her feet lay the little flute. She grabbed it. Alone again, she turned and ran from Crowninshield's woods as though the Dark One was right behind her.

2

Something touched my arm.

"Wha-a-a-t?" I woke up, breathing hard. What was it, that faceless man reaching for my wrist again? My heart pounded so hard it hurt.

"G'amma says get up. G'amma says get up *now*!"

Just my three-year-old niece Gracey. The dream faded and I relaxed. A nightmare, that's all. I was home in my own bed on a hot September morning, not stuck in the mud of some smelly marsh. But then I groaned, still tired. I had school today.

I hadn't gotten much sleep. All night long, the Santa Ana winds had blown in from California's deserts, rattling every window in the house. Right now, their dry heat made my room an oven. They weren't called Devil Winds for nothing.

Devil Winds. Of course. That's why I'd dreamed a weird dream about demons and witches. I didn't believe in stuff like that, and Halloween, when everything eerie was fake, was more than a month away. Yeah, the Devil Winds made me do it.

My heartbeat settled back to normal. I just wanted to climb deep inside the covers, but it was way too hot. September is the cruelest month. After I get to sleep late all summer and lay out on a cool beach, school definitely stinks. But it's way worse now with the new headmaster. Over the summer, he replaced two teachers we all really liked with the favorites he had

11

brought with him.

Yeah. St. Bartholomew the Great's Preparatory School was the last place I wanted to go these days. At least I got to be with my friends, even though Abby sure seemed more mischievous than ever. Kind of a spoiled brat, she sure knew which buttons to push. But her dad was head of the St. Bart's Board of Trustees, so no one ever messed with her.

My little niece babbled; she was so cute. Mostly I enjoy having her around. I have a whole herd of siblings, but they're all pretty much grown up because my parents got an early start and had me last. So far, I've spent most of my life sort of like an only child. But right now my sister Angie is back home with her two little girls while her husband's deployed in the Middle East monitoring and controlling air space.

"Come on, sleepyhead." Angie's voice was very mother-like as she swooped into the room. "Although *somebody* didn't feel the need to do laundry this weekend, I found it in my heart to wash your gym clothes for you. I delivered you from demerits." She blinked her eyes really fast at me. "Deliverance, dear."

"Don't call me that," I grumped. It reminded me too much of my dream. Our parents didn't do anything mainstream. Not even naming their kids, but everybody always called me Delli. I was grateful, though, for Angie's loving care. "Thanks. I mean it. Bible study ran later than usual last night. We're already planning the Spring Sing." I couldn't help laughing a little.

But then my bad mood came back. Having to wear a uniform was lame enough, but now I had to climb into a St. Bart's ugly maroon and yellow plaid skirt at home then change into P.E. clothes ten seconds after the Pledge to Allegiance.

I might even have liked the new headmaster if he had even read our petition. We wanted to be allowed to come to school in our P.E. clothes. But no. That wasn't proper. Appearance was everything. His word was law. No one else's opinions counted. Never ever.

"Breakfast." My mom's voice rang through the house. You should know she doesn't like being called "Mom." Mostly it's Mattie now, but she'll answer to Blooming Iris from the old days when she and dad were vagabonds and hippies.

I tried not to imagine the cuisine downstairs. Mom, well, Mattie always preaches that white flour and white sugar are true poison, caffeine a close third. I'd just about hurled yesterday at a batch of muffins made from olive oil and wheat germ. And I was totally sick of chamomile tea.

By now, I knew my dad was busy doing something in the avocado groves with Hank, his handyman. Wind and the damage it can cause is something avocado growers live with, but I figured he'd need a hug, anyway.

At home I call my parents by their first names although around my friends I call them Mom and Dad like a normal kid. But Chris and Mattie only. I don't *ever* say White Sage or Blooming Iris.

When I thought about the muffins, I figured I could convince Angie to stop by the Coffee 'n' Cruller near school. We'd both be better off starting our day with the jolt of a *latte* and a maple nut scone than anything our mom cooked up. I couldn't get my driver's license until I turned sixteen in December, and I liked Angie's Accord much more than my dad's old pickup.

"No thanks, Mattie," I yelled, and Angie and I both rolled our eyes. But instead of leaving me my privacy, Angie started puttering around the bedroom. It was horribly annoying. Angie wanted to "earn her keep" by tidying the house. Mattie is a terrible housekeeper since she doesn't really believe in material possessions. But my room is *my* space. Plus I don't like people watching me change clothes. I'd have to do that soon enough in the P.E. locker room. Yuck.

"Sheesh! What happened to your shoes?" Angie called out like *she'd* paid for them or something. Or had to scrape them clean now when I totally expected to do it. "It's dry as a bone out, but you look like you hiked through a swamp."

Swamp. She lifted up my sneakers. They were practically brand new since school had barely started.

My brand new white sneakers totally encrusted with dried mud.

My skin scrawled. I couldn't help but remember the stinky mud sucking at my feet in the dream.

Well, the dream girl's feet, that is.

"And this!" As Angie bent down to pick up something off the floor, her voice rose to a high note of disapproval. I couldn't even hear the wind over it.

"Oh, no. Sorry." Angie blushed, "I...thought you might be smoking something you shouldn't."

Between her fingers, Angie held up something shaped like a big cigarette.

I was so totally outraged. Whatever their youth had been like (they kind of looked the part), our folks had brought us up completely against abusing substances. Or even smoking.

"Hmm. It's a little flute of some kind," she announced, peering closely at it. "Why, this is too cute.

Handmade from a reed or something. Did you make this in Handicrafts class?"

My heart started to beat so fast I thought I would die.

Ten minutes later I was ready to go—I'm a fast dresser and showered after P.E, anyway, I didn't even mention stopping at the coffee shop. My brain was aching, because normally, I didn't have to think too hard. Other than homework, which I'm good at because I'm an honor student, I rarely pondered anything of substance, and, if I'm honest, I never thought about anything *too hard* (except maybe how to earn a little extra money). Never even worried much about what to wear, what with St. Bart's uniforms and all that.

But, the dream? I have to admit, the dream, and the dream-flute in real time, was all making me a little crazy—and not in a crazy-good way.

During homeroom, I attempted to calm down. There were always reasonable explanations for everything. Somehow, I'd gotten my shoes dirty and forgotten about it. After all, I did have lots of shoes. Mostly from discount stores, not designer brands, but they still counted. Maybe these weren't even my new shoes. I'd rushed a lot this morning.

The awful Santa Ana winds did dry everything out, so maybe my dad and Hank had irrigated the avocado grove, and I'd stepped in a mud puddle they'd made.

Yeah, and that's why I had that dream about mud sucking at my feet. Of course. My breathing slowed.

And the flute. Why, probably my dad or Hank made it for my nieces. That's it!

After I slammed my locker shut and headed

toward the gym, I felt so much better that I wished we'd stopped for the latte.

My very best friend Abby Goodman was already dressed in her P.E. clothes. The collared polo shirt didn't have the school-logo we were supposed to wear, but Abby wouldn't get any demerits for it. She led a charmed life, that girl.

"Dad's going to see that Mr. Scatabello fires her, that's for sure!" As she talked, Abby scraped her long golden hair into a scrunchied ponytail. It was cinched so tight that from the front she looked bald, but she'd be hot-looking anyway with or without real hair.

"Fire who?" I asked the rapt throng. I admit to feeling a pang of envy at that hair. My own hair is a whole bunch of different shades of copper and bronze, and overall it's all right. I do tend to get lots of compliments on it. But it frizzes so bad in the dry winds I could remove rust with it.

"Ms. Lipsett," whispered Betsy Barich, my second-best buddy, in a kind of hiss.

"What on earth for?" Ms. Lipsett, our Ethics and Morality teacher, put to rest the stereotype of geeky high school teacher. She could have been a supermodel. Instead, she was a Rhodes Scholar who taught at a prep school.

Abby turned to me. "Daddy went out with friends on Saturday night and saw it in person. Her! *Ms. Lipsett is a barmaid!*" she said in a loud dramatic whisper.

"You mean topless?"

"No, silly," Abby pouted. "Daddy doesn't go to places like that! But he said she had on a miniskirt up to here." She laid her hand sideways high on her thigh, "and a croppy top. And she has a *belly ring!*"

She made the last two words sound downright

dirty, but I didn't think a belly ring was so scandalous. Angie and my other sisters Patience and Peony have had them forever. As for me, the process seems too painful, the results hard to keep clean, and nothing I ever even want to try. But I felt the need to defend the procedure anyway.

"Well, my sisters have belly rings. And you've been yelling you want one. What's the big deal?" I shrugged.

"It isn't about the *ring*, Delli." Abby's nose rose high in the air. "Your *sisters* aren't representatives of St. Bartholomew the Great's Prep School. *They* aren't molding impressionable teenage minds."

I climbed into my own polo shirt. That sure didn't sound like Abby talking. She was the only person who molded her own mind. "Well, I don't see why you've got your panties in a knot," I told her even though the fabric muffled my words while I pulled the shirt on. "She's a great teacher. I had her last year."

"That's just the point," Betsy stated firmly, nodding at Abby. "Ms. Lipsett teaches Ethics and Morality. How on earth can she do that if she's a *barmaid*?"

The entire gym class started moving their chins up and down along with Abby and Betsy. It was all I could do to keep my own head still. Maybe Abby was right. I thought hard for a minute. Well, maybe if prospective parents knew Ms. Lipsett pranced about a bar with a lot of skin showing, they might not want to enroll their kids.

Maybe.

And all the donors who supplied funds for athletics and computers and Fine Arts, well, what if they found her actions inappropriate? The school could be out gobs of money.

I started my stretches and shrugged again. But then some odd words wiggled throughout my brain, words I thought I'd forgotten.

God will give you blood to drink.

3

I tried to forget the words and relieve my tense muscles by actually playing speedball out on the soccer field. The morning wasn't too hot yet. Some dew still covered the grass. Every time the ball came my way, I kicked it to kingdom come. The red rubber ball was the same kind we'd played with in kindergarten.

Like usual, Abby and Betsy stood moaning on the sidelines near the bleachers. They always worried they'd mess up their manicures.

Finally, Coach Clayter replaced me with someone else, and I headed toward my friends.

All of a sudden the coach burst out in laughter, pointing at my muddy sneakers. The wet grass hadn't done them any favors. "Hey, Willis, what'd you do? Go four-wheeling with your feet?"

I laughed, too, but Abby tossed the P.E. teacher a dark look.

"Get 'em spic and span before tomorrow. We gotta keep that field clean." She laughed again. When Coach Clayter turned back to her clipboard, Abby shoved over to me.

"How dare that woman humiliate you like that." Her well-glossed lips barely moved over clenched teeth. "Harassment's against the law!"

Like always, Betsy nodded in full agreement.

I was stunned. "Humiliate me? Abby, she was just teasing. Angie laughed about them, too. Coach didn't mean anything."

Abby sniffed. "She has no right to comment on anything we do. Or wear." She ground her teeth. "Or worse, laugh at us!"

I rolled my eyes. "Get a life, Abs. She's our teacher. It's her job to comment. She could have given me demerits. I'm sure my shoes don't exactly qualify as 'white' today."

"She serves us, Delli. We pay her. That comment was just not right."

"Well, no big deal. I'd get over it if I were you." I shook my head and started off toward the locker room.

Abby huffed to my side. "Well, you're not me. Coach Clayter is wrong. Plain and simple."

"Aw, Abs." I heard my own moan.

"Besides, she insults us by making us play little kids' games," Betsy threw in. "What's with speedball? Why can't we play actual soccer?"

"Besides," Abby repeated then announced, "we don't need showers. *Showers are a requirement.*" She mimicked Coach Clayter pretty well. "I've got lavender water we can spritz on. French, by the way."

Well, as for me, a shower felt good. Maybe the lavender water relaxed Abby and Betsy and the rest of the gaggle because everybody seemed friends again by the time I'd dried and dressed and the bell rang to change classes.

I groaned. Next was American Lit, my hardest class even with Physics in the mix. Normally I liked getting it over with early in the day, but I really didn't want to face Mr. Gallindo. He had been around forever and knew every trick.

If you waltzed into class confident, looking him right in the eye, he called on you. If you tried to sneak past him and avoid eye contact, he called on you. He called on you when you had memorized every page, and he called on you when you knew nothing at all.

And today of course, I knew nothing at all. Normally I did, but today was one of those rare days when I didn't.

There was no escape. Well, not yet anyway. Abby's scuttlebutt seemed to think that Headmaster Anthony Scatabello, otherwise known as Scat, wanted to force Mr. Gallindo's retirement, but avoided bad blood by letting him finish out the year. Mr. Gallindo had been at the school about forty years, and the alumni and boosters loved him. Way lots more than anybody loved Scat. (Yes, we all knew it means animal dung.)

"Hey, did we have American Lit homework?" I asked Abby, pretty worried. "I wasn't here on Friday. I had that student council leadership day at Pepperdine."

I should have asked somebody. I could have, and I always did. All juniors took the class, and whatever period you had it, the assignment schedule was the same. But this once, I hadn't asked.

Abby shrugged. "I don't know. Without you here, I didn't want to come to school. So I stayed home. Anyway, I don't have him until last period. I can probably do whatever it is during lunch. I'm going to see the counselor now."

"Counselor? Why?"

But Abby had already vanished into the sea of maroon and yellow plaid that dammed up the hall.

"We had to read the background pages. About some witch trials," Betsy offered helpfully. "You won't be excused from reading it. He assigned it on Thursday because a lot of people would be gone on Friday. Not that I really read it. I just looked at the bold type."

Thursday? My heart sank. Usually I paid better attention. Of course, nobody's perfect, but I was at St. Bart's on academic scholarship.

"Someplace called Salem," somebody else said.

My ears began to ring with sounds from another life. The world around me seemed to morph into slow motion.

"Salem Village?" The words came out of my mouth with hardly any sound.

Betsy shrugged, "I don't know about any village, but it's Salem for sure."

~AΩ~

I didn't know the answer to Mr. Gallindo's question—what year—but Betsy did. It had obviously been bold-faced somewhere in the pages she'd skimmed.

She sing-songed 1692, like little kids did with Christopher Columbus and 1492 and the ocean blue.

But the class stalled after that. Except for me. I who hadn't read a thing.

"Well, in what month was the first so-called witch executed?" Old Gallindo rarely left his desk, but that didn't matter. He had all-seeing eyeballs, and above all, all-hearing ears. Pretty good senses for an old guy.

I knew. *I knew!* I could see his brown-eyed glare from behind his glasses. From underneath a gray caterpillar of a brow. He knew that I knew. But I didn't know how I knew. Well, I knew how. The dream. I just didn't know *why*.

"June. A tavern owner. A woman." I mumbled. I

mean, I was right but it wouldn't be a good idea to seem too confident.

His face practically split open with joy. "Right on, girl. Speak up. What was her name? What was her crime?"

I couldn't remember the name. Pastor? Preacher? Something churchy. But I did know she hadn't done witchcraft. "She didn't commit much of a crime as far as I can see," I replied, honestly "She knew the Scriptures, and she nursed the sick. I guess she just didn't worship in their way."

He was nodding. "Yes. The Puritans had very strict codes of belief and behavior and an endless work ethic."

I remembered the heavy dark skirts catching in the mud. "And she dressed in pretty clothes. Scarlet. With lace. They, the Puritans I guess, considered that frivolous."

"Naah," a boy guffawed without raising his hand, "For that she got hung for witchcraft?"

I looked at him, then back at Mr. Gallindo. My confidence was growing. "Even godly people died. Folks like Goodwife Nurse."

God will give you blood to drink. I remembered the woman from my dream. The one who had brought smallpox and filth and laziness into her community.

Who had cursed the judge who condemned her.

I went on. "Or folks who were dirty and lazy. One old homeless woman cursed the judge. She said God would give him blood to drink if she was hanged."

Mr. Gallindo's lower jaw dropped and looked bigger than ever was clearly amazed. His eyebrows climbed up his forehead. Obviously, that wasn't in the homework reading. "Why, yes, Delli. Only Sarah Good wasn't all that old. She had a little daughter who was accused of witchcraft, too."

"But why?" the boy persisted. I didn't turn around, but I think it was Corey Mergen. His mom was the counselor.

I suspected why. The homeless woman didn't fit in, and my skin crawled, some of it relief. Fitting in with the rich kids at St. Bart's was hard, but I always had. Poor Mrs. Pastor-Preacher, too, in her scarlet and lace. At least wearing uniforms spared those of us who couldn't afford The Gap.

Or was it Goodwife? Goodwife Preacher-Pastor. What did that dumb term mean?

Right now, though, it was hard to accept I'd had a dream that meant something. It had never happened before. Mr. Gallindo looked at me hopefully, but I shook my head. My heart beat funny, and I needed to end my fifteen-seconds of Gallindo glory.

I shrugged my shoulders to notify him that my supply of knowledge had been depleted. Certainly I'd earned enough brown-noser points today to start acting bored.

But I really felt creeped out. My heart thrashed even faster, and now I was finding it hard to breathe. Why had I had a dream that sort of came true?

Maybe I should ask for the bathroom pass. My tummy was queasy. But I had no need, though.

At that exact second, an office aide came into the room with a pass for me to the headmaster's office. The class all uh-ohed like I was in trouble. I wasn't, but I was still wiggy. This was one of those days when normal people shouldn't have gotten out of bed, but actually, that was where all my troubles had started.

Before I got up to leave, Mr. Gallindo told the class

solemnly, "Some bored young girls started it all, the witch hunts in Salem. Young girls whose parents believed they could do no wrong because they had been brought up so properly."

~AΩ~

Both Coach Clayter and Mrs. Mergen, the school counselor watched nervously as I entered the room. I'd prayed the whole way from class. I just wasn't one of those that ever got in trouble. Then it dawned on me. This wasn't about me. It was about Abby.

A bored young girl whose parents believed she could do no wrong.

But I loved Abby. I would never betray her. Deep down, Abby had a good heart. She'd befriended me my first day at St. Bart's when I didn't know anybody. Her mom had recently abandoned the family, and Abby was having a really hard time with it. Besides, she sure was generous.

Mr. Scatabello tried to act imposing, but he had a bald spot he tried to hide, which just made him look dumb. Plus he was too small of a man to appear significant. Maybe that's why he made so many bad decisions, just because he had the power to do so.

"Delli, please, sit down."

Although I wanted to stand up just to be ornery, my legs were too rubbery—some from playing speedball but most due to the weird things that had gone on since I woke up. I wouldn't dare get Abby into trouble, but I sure would support Coach Clayter.

I said hello to the two women faculty members, and each returned a shaky smile.

"Delli." The headmaster tried to add a boom to his

voice, but I wasn't at all impressed. Even when he used a loudspeaker or microphone, he sounded like a dweeb. "We've had a report that during first period P.E. today, several students witnessed Coach Clayter harassing you, humiliating you, over what you were wearing."

I gave the coach what I hoped was a confident smile.

"That's not true. Coach was joking about my muddy shoes." Then an inspiration hit me. "Coach was real cool about it. She could have given me demerits because they technically weren't white. She was *way* cool about it."

The headmaster swung his head back and forth with really jerky motions as his glare hopped between me and the coach. All I could think of was a TV special on time-lapse photography Mattie had made me watch once. His entire body quivered so much I thought his head would pop right off his neck. I had to cough to hold back laughing out loud in his face. Then I saw his stupid comb-over from the back and coughed harder.

I stood my ground. "I don't see how it would have bothered anybody. 'Specially, if it didn't bother Coach or me."

"Well, we all must be on the lookout for improper behavior. That's one of the unspoken responsibilities of *all* who participate in the St. Bartholomew environment." He was so pompous I wanted to smack him. He didn't mean "all" at all. He meant people who had influence.

"If you don't mind, I'd like to know who reported this 'incident,'" I said casually.

Scat's eyes opened wide. They did that sometimes, both when he was trying to be cool around the seniors and when he was trying to be intense.

"I'm not at liberty to say. The report was submitted anonymously in the suggestion box." Scat cleared his throat, to make his voice deeper, I guessed. "The report indicated that several students were troubled by the incident. Perhaps *you* know who they might be? Who in that class seemed upset by Coach Clayter's supposed joke?"

I shrugged. Of course I knew, but I played innocent. I wasn't about to get Abby and Betsy involved. I'd yell at them plenty later about trying to act all big and powerful, especially about something that didn't bother me one single bit.

I unclenched my fists. "I don't have any problem with Coach Clayter. She's great. But permission to speak freely, sir." I hated to call him "sir," but I had heard that line in a movie recently and wanted to use it somehow.

He nodded.

I continued, "A lot of us wish the suggestion box was like...before. When you had to sign your name and put your student I.D. number. It just...seemed more honest somehow."

Scat stood up then, clearly annoyed and way too short for a grown-up. "This is the way it was done at my old school. I find it highly effective. I'm not willing to discuss it. Well, ladies, perhaps this meeting is over." He touched his hand somewhat nervously to his dumb bald spot, like he was hoping it was still covered.

Or maybe wasn't there anymore.

He took his hand away finally and went on with his orders. "Coach Clayter, please watch what you say. On the outside chance that some other day, you may let slip something that *does* offend someone, somehow. Miss Willis, you may return to class."

The bell starting the fifteen-minute nutrition period rang just then, and I ran to the cafeteria to tear into Abby. At least my anger had displaced the creepiness coursing in my veins.

I grabbed her arm. "What on earth do you think you're doing, trying to get Coach Clayter into trouble?"

Abby gave me a satisfied smirk. "Well, obviously she isn't in trouble, thanks to you. What's the big deal?

"*What's the big deal?* Being a tattletale is a big deal. You've known that since like second grade," I shot back.

"I'm not tattling. She has no right to laugh at her students. She's lucky she didn't do that to me." Abby tucked her long blonde hair behind lobes stuck with diamond studs. "If she had, she'd be talking to Daddy's attorney now instead of Scat."

I didn't reply because Abby never listened unless she wanted to. And she was right. It was better the stupid incident had involved me, because my parents were very tolerant about both big and little things. Until I was two, they'd traveled to many countries, teaching English as a second language. They'd learned to appreciate different cultures and philosophies, and during those explorations, they found the one true God and His Son Jesus. They'd always adhered to His commandment, "Love your neighbor as yourself" and taught us kids the same. For a moment, I surged with love for Chris and Mattie. Sometimes it was a good thing to have oddballs for parents.

But Abby needed to know that I had protected her as well. "FYI, he tried to get me to rat *you* out," I told her, seriously holding back a smirk. "It's also part of his job to find out who is accusing one of his teachers. Making stuff up, telling lies. Stuff like that."

For a second, Abby looked alarmed. "What did you say?"

I had to smirk now. "I don't name names."

Just then, Betsy came up from the counter with two clear plastic glasses, thrusting one into Abby's hand, holding the other up to my lips.

"It's tomato juice. Abs says we gotta start eating and drinking more healthy stuff."

The red liquid touched my mouth.

God will give you blood to drink.

Suddenly, I gagged. There was nothing in my stomach, but I managed to get to a stall in the girls' room before I started to retch.

Over and over again.

4

After getting sick, I waited in the school office for nearly an hour. Angie came in finally, apologizing. "Mattie's got a conference call going with Pendant Press"—our mom runs a small bookstore downtown—"and Chris, he's deep into tending the groves."

When I was two, he'd inherited the place from his uncle Ted and resigned from his last school. He's still credentialed, a good man and smart, but he's just better without a suit and tie and four walls. So the avocado venture came at the right time. Then came El Nino, a series of severe winter storms that trashes coastal California every once in a while. He never talks money, but I think he's still recovering. Nobody wastes growing space on windbreaks. Growers take their chances with wind damage.

"Don't be sorry. I'm glad it's you," I told my sister weakly, but I meant it. Abby had looked terrified while Betsy, pale with giant eyes, had run for the school nurse. I guess I must have carried on pretty badly, and my mom is never good in a crisis.

"Listen, sweetie." Angie's eyes were big with concern. "You're not...I mean, you could tell *me*. You know I can keep a secret. You know that."

What was Angie thinking?

"No, I'm not *pregnant*." I spat, insulted. "I've taken a purity vow. Besides which, I'm not stupid. It's because of the heat. And I ran a lot during P.E."

Angie turned purple. "Well, I had to ask. It'd be better coming from me than Mom or Dad. I noticed that you didn't eat anything this morning or ask to stop at the coffee shop." She wrapped her arm securely around my middle as she supported me to the car. Her hands were gentle, and I didn't miss my mom as much.

But I was still offended by her question. "Mom and Dad know me. They'd never ask any such thing."

"Well, bad things can happen to good girls," Angie insisted, buckling me in like I was two. She was clearly embarrassed, though. "Now once we get home, I'll get you some tea. Yes, real pekoe tea. Sweetened with real, awful, white sugar. And you can have some soda crackers made with white flour! And some totally wicked commercially prepared strawberry jam! "

I smiled a little. This was heresy indeed.

"That helps settle nausea. The only way I got through the morning sickness with McKenna." Angie's voice stumbled, embarrassed again.

We drove off.

"It's just so interesting..." She chuckled, normal again. "You know, our anti-establishment parents are sending you to a prep school."

I still felt weak and shaky and not much like chatting, but Angie was awfully nice. Even if she had thought even for a second that I could be, well.

"I got a great scholarship," I said.

"And St. Bart's is closer and, well, being closer sure makes days like today easier on everybody," Angie soothed as she braked. For once, we hit a red light at Baldwin Crossing. "By the way, I made your bed after you left and cleaned up a little. You sure live in a sty."

"Gee, thanks," I told her, not really meaning it

because of the sty remark.

"The linens will be cool and clean. I even rubbed baby powder between the sheets. You'll sleep like a newborn."

Sleep. That's just what I needed. After my heretical snack of course.

"Hey, thanks, Ange." I really did mean this. The baby part sounded good. Babies didn't have bad dreams, did they? I was awfully tired, but home again. Nice. I brushed my teeth long and hard. At least the normal taste was back in my mouth. Then I had a snack and brushed them again.

Angie was right. The cool clean sheets felt like heaven against my skin. And the smell of baby powder replaced the scent of the tomato juice that for whatever reason still hung in my nose. *God will give you*...no, I stopped my brain from reciting the mantra again.

I puffed up the pillow then raked my long tangly hair across it like a fan as I laid down my head, to keep my neck cool.

"Sweetheart." My mom's voice was soothing as she walked in. So was the hand she laid on my cheek. "I'm so sorry, but I had no choice but to take the call. My main supplier. Sweetheart, sweetheart." She bent to kiss me and her own long hair tickled my cheek.

My mom's hairstyle hasn't changed for forty years, I guess. Parted in the middle, it hangs past her waist like those folk singers from long ago. It's been pewter gray as long as I can remember, but everything about it suits her.

"No problem, Mom. Mattie. Mommy. I'm safe now." I smiled at her before I closed my eyes.

The mask of sleep seemed to cover me just like the cool blankets. But all of a sudden, I stood on a porch.

The porch of a well-tended saltbox house.

The well-tended house was as fine as the home of Francis and Rebecca Nurse and certainly one to be envied. It was Deliverance's home, and she didn't remember walking up the steps to it. Nerves tumbled down her back. She feared to face what was on the other side of the door. One of these days, when she returned home from an errand in the village, she would find their house empty. She would find that her honored mother had been "named" by one of the afflicted girls and remanded to the prison as a witch.

Or worse, she would find that her small sister had been declared the demon seed of a spectral rape and taken away.

Was today the day?

Her mother sat, busy stitching at the hearth. Relief nearly buckled Deliverance's knees. She needed normality especially now that the stranger in the woods had said he would find her.

Oddly, she wasn't afraid anymore. Of him, at least. But she was foolish, for she longed to see him again. To talk with him. To listen to the little flute.

To have him kiss her wrist.

She blushed furiously. Longing for the physical touch of a man not one's husband was wanton.

"Sweeting, sweeting!" Her mother's relief soon turned to unhappiness. "God give me strength, Deliverance! Where have you been? These are not times to be out and about after dark!"

Even as she scolded, prim and disapproving, she was still a beauty. Deliverance loved her dearly.

"I am home and well, honored mother..."

"You're a slattern, Deliverance!" Her mother chided. "Where have you been gadding?"

The disapproval met Deliverance like a slap. Indeed, the mad run from the woods had soiled her white smock with mud. Thorns had ripped her dark skirt.

"My honored mother, my errand was a good one. I stopped for feverfew for Patience in Goodman Crowninshield's woods. But I forgot the time and ran the whole way home. It was getting dark." Like a child much younger than her fifteen years, Deliverance scrubbed her hands against her skirt.

Her mother's disfavor seemed to melt. Neither of them mentioned the hungry wolves that were said to prowl the forests.

"Well, truth to tell, God is nearby, but so are those who wish harm to the innocent. Dearest, these are simply not times to be about. Go wash."

Deliverance silenced her footsteps across the puncheon floor. Although her mother busied herself cutting bread and cheese, Deliverance suspected she really wanted to talk.

"Dear Mother, before I visited the marsh, I did stop for a chat with Mary." Ah. She remembered where she'd been. Giddy, she sank down upon the rough-hewn plank her good father had once fashioned into a bench.

"Mary?"

"Mary Warren. You know full well." Deliverance tried to speak in a lighthearted way, but she could see the worry adding years to her mother's face.

"Mary Warren will cause nothing but trouble," her mother said stiffly. "She is one of *those girls!*"

Deliverance knew her mother meant no insult. The circle girls were a group to be feared. Yet...Deliverance felt stubborn.

"Those girls are my friends," she said.

"Then be careful!" Suddenly her mother stopped, lost in thought. Her white-capped head began to nod. "No, daughter. Mayhap it is wisdom to keep them as friends. Particularly young Ann Putnam. Their approval might keep us safe."

As Deliverance looked up with silent questions, fear nudged her heart.

Her mother sighed. "I sometimes feel a threat. 'Tis a year soon that your father left this earth for heaven. 'Tis the proper waiting time for some widowed farmer or bachelor to press for my hand."

Deliverance shrugged. That would not be irregular.

"*To gain our farm, silly goose!*" Her mother's voice rose impatiently. "I've no wish for a new man. But if I refuse him, just think how the accusations might fly about Salem Village!"

"Dear mother, surely not! You are truly respected, as was my father!" Deliverance half-rose, holding off a shudder.

"No more respected than Goody Nurse." Matilda's voice began to shake. "Lean close, girl. I will never say these words out loud again, but Rebecca Nurse was condemned only because Goodman Putnam desires her property. Plus she has long been at odds with Reverend Parris. We must tread with care. If I were named a witch, Deliverance, your father's land would be forfeit!" She set down the long knife and stared at the fire.

Deliverance's knees weakened even as she rose to

embrace her mother. "Mother, no..."

"Deliverance, you must know this. Even if I select some good man as my husband, he would surely want this farm for his own heirs. And that means..."

That meant Deliverance and Patience would be in danger, too.

Her honored mother mumbled softly, "Oh, that our firstborn son Welcome had not died before his time. He would be a man by now. And his twin Anguish would be a woman grown, mayhap with a powerful husband to protect us."

Deliverance had long known how the loss of the twins had broken her mother's heart despite the deep faith and later daughters that granted her comfort. She drew her mother close. "Now, honored mother, let us not think on such things. Surely, this evil time will be over soon."

"Such is my hope." Mother sighed. "But keep on good terms with Mary, with Ann and... with all the circle girls. They just might be our liberation. If...if..." Her mother's broke like glass.

"All right. Indeed, I will. I promise." Deliverance felt a rush of care. She would not fret her mother. She would court the wily girls and claim to be their friend.

However, she had to tell her mother of what Mary Warren had confided. "Mother, dear mother." Her voice lowered as she pulled her mother close again. "In truth, Mary is troubled by the accusations. She whispers that the girls practice foolery with their fits and only pretend to see visions of demons. She longs to convince them to halt."

Mother almost shrieked. "Stop. Then perhaps it is best to stay away! I want to hear no more! These are deadly times, Deliverance. We cannot be observed to be suspicious. And now you wander through the woods, alone, in the gloaming where the reverend reputes that the Dark One lives. Did anyone see you?"

Did anyone see me?

Deliverance didn't say anything. How could she tell her mother about the strangely beautiful young man that she wanted to see again? She couldn't. That way her own words could not come back to haunt either of them.

"Let me tend Patience so that you can have your evening to yourself and your prayers, dear mother. I know how hard Goody Nurse's death has hurt you."

But her mother's face turned pale. She was still clearly troubled. "Did anyone see you?" In her agitation, she reached for Deliverance's hand, her fingers almost like claws.

"What—what's this, daughter?" Her hand was work worn but still looked girlish in many ways. Her fingers rubbed at something at Deliverance's wrist.

Confused, Deliverance looked down.

A red mark. Where the young man had laid his lips at her wrist.

A frigid heat clamped her spine. "Oh, I must have scraped myself on a bramble or some such." Hiding her alarm, Deliverance explained mildly in spite of her hammering heart.

"But the skin isn't torn. Oh, God be merciful! Deliverance, the wound looks not unlike...the partial marks of a kiss." She struggled to speak the intimate word. "Oh, *a witch's kiss!* That's what they will say! Your bramble has left you with a witch's mark! Deliverance, pray that it heals soon."

But Deliverance didn't want it gone. Until she could find the man again. How strange. Not a half hour had passed since she ran from him in fear. Now she longed to see him again, to find out his secrets. What had happened to his face? From whence had he come?

Instead she nodded, reaching for a slice of bread and a hunk of cheese. She was amazingly hungry, like she hadn't eaten all day. Which was absurd. Even in lean times, her mother set a healthy table. Then her mother's voice was sharp again.

"Deliverance? Where is your cap? Did you leave it on the porch?" Obviously, she had not forgotten the gossip about Deliverance's hell-fire hair. Besides, a bare head was unseemly and immodest.

Marks of true suspicion.

Deliverance's heart stopped for a second. Her mother had every reason to be alarmed. What if someone nosy and troublesome, someone like Goody Putnam or someone who wanted their farm, had seen her just now? Seen her fiery hair streaking behind her...then found her cap blowing in the wind like a sprite...

"It blew off as I ran," Deliverance replied, now completely contrite. On top of the fear, she knew that her mother despised wastefulness. "I reached for it, but..."

Her excuse was lame.

"Never-the-mind." Her mother sighed once again. "I have another in my chest. But love, if someone finds it, I hope it is not identified as yours." Her pretty brow furrowed for a moment then she brightened. "Ah, sweeting, forgive my worries! I wish again that we could leave here. In good times, the farm is prosperous, but now it has fallen fallow and untended. You and I do what we can, true, but I cannot get workers to hire. Not when everyone attends the trials each day. We could not get in a sale near what your father would have deemed worthy..."

Such was true. All summer, the horrible accusations by and against neighbors as well as the afflictions of the girls had kept farmers from their fields, goodwives from their gardens. Besides, everyone knew that the devil could allow no food to grow.

Only Divine Providence knew how Salem households would eat come winter. Other than the Wyllyses perhaps. Deliverance almost smiled when she thought of Goody Putnam hinting that she was slothful. She and her mother had managed to maintain their garden and preserve the food. They had clipped the sheep and tended the flax and brewed the cider. They would have food, beverage, and warm clothes. They had put in long, weary hours past eventide because they still attended the trials all day. To stay away from the court would have aroused suspicions.

So Deliverance had little to worry about. She was not slothful. She could take time to dream about a flute player in the forest who had kissed her.

"Come, sit here." Her mother's voice was soft with demand. "Let's take care of that hair." She dragged a whalebone comb through the tangled mess. The tugs hurt, but Deliverance didn't complain. She deserved it for being careless with the cap that kept her neat and modest. Soon, the glowing mess lay tamed in a long rope of braid down her back.

In a daring whimsy, her mother tied a ribbon to the end of the plait.

Just then, came an unexpected knock on the door.

Mother and daughter stiffened as one. The sound

made them imagine the worst: The constable with an accusation on his lips and a warrant in his hand.

"Our Father in heaven." Her mother bowed her head as she pointed. Deliverance groaned, too. Patience's cornhusk dolls sat in a little family by the fire.

Poppets. The afflicted girls had used poppets to doom Elizabeth Procter. Testimony claimed they were ritual devices that witches used to torture the innocent.

Deliverance hid the little flute in the folds of her dress. Fear drenched her armpits. The knocking grew insistent.

The sound grew louder.

~AΩ~

"Delli? *Delli*?" Abby and Betsy called out as one as they banged on my bedroom door.

Startled, I shot up to a sitting position. For a second, I felt confusion, almost terror. Then I realized that I'd just had another dream.

Just a dream. I was back in my bedroom. In my own world. With my friends. I'd gotten sick at school, that's all.

Relief swarmed over my skin like a suntan.

"Hey, we came to see how you are." Betsy held out a little bunch of flowers.

"Dang, sweet braid!" Abby was actually gentle as she shook the long line of hair hanging down my back.

5

Abby and Betsy were screeching loudly at how clean my room was. I hardly heard them, pulling instead at the braid. My world wasn't my own after all.

How on earth had it happened? As I mentioned earlier, my hair was always a tangled mass when the Santa Ana's blew, taking the humidity to zero. Then I calmed down, feeling warm and sunny again. I figured it all out.

While I slept, I'd braided my hair while the dream mother braided her daughter's. Of course! Sort of like someone sleepwalking. In fact, it all made perfect sense. I had French-braided little Gracey's hair just before Sunday school yesterday morning. Braids must have remained in my subconscious.

When my heartbeat slowed, I teased Abby about my clean room. "Well, not all of us are rich and have maids."

Betsy's lips turned out in dismay as she pointed to Abby. "That's Miss Priss over there. I'm not rich. My dad's a fireman."

"Well, at least the pay is stable." I gestured vaguely toward the window. "It sure beats nature beating your trees to death."

Neither of my visitors said anything until Abby complained. "It's hot in here. Don't you have air conditioning?"

Abby annoyed me. She just didn't get it. Not

everyone was rich with the latest everything. "No. We don't have air conditioning. My great uncle Ted built this house when he married Aunt Jeanette and that was, like, fifty years ago. We could go outside."

"Nah. It's just as hot out there."

Well, I would have liked some fresh air, but Abby was a guest after all. How long had I been asleep anyway? That had been a full-on dream. Suddenly I was annoyed even more at Abby and Betsy for waking me up. Who was at Deliverance's door? The constable to arrest her for her hell-fire hair? For meeting with a demon in the swamp?

To name her mother a witch so someone could claim the farm?

Or had the faceless man found her? Besides, the bread and cheese had looked good.

Funny, the man in the swamp didn't make *me* want to see him again. He sort of creeped me out. But then, I saw normal cute guys every day. I got the impression from the dreams that Puritan girls didn't get to hang out with members of the opposite sex. Maybe that was why Deliverance had seemed so eager, so jazzed about that weird kiss. Suddenly I remembered to check inside of my wrist.

Nothing. That was something. I actually felt the sunglow of relief again.

"Why doesn't your dad just sell this land?" Abby wasn't finished. "He could make a fortune. Cut down all those trees and you'd probably have a bit of an ocean view. That says 'luxury condo complex.'"

I wanted to be rude and tell her to be quiet. My dad would never sell this place. Would never *ever* cut down the trees. But instead I asked, "Did you guys cut class? You know Scat hates that."

Both sneered at me. "It's after four o'clock."

Crazy! I had slept most of the day away.

Abby opened her mouth to speak, waving both hands the way she does when something was very important, but Angie interrupted her. "I'm bringing you all a snack."

"Uh, no, it's OK," I called back, thinking of the wheat germ and olive oil muffins, and horrible smoothies made from carrots and peas. I *was* hungry but not for stuff that would make me hurl again.

"No worries. Doughnuts and cola. Sugar and all."

Then I thought about the bread and cheese and how I hadn't eaten anything but crackers all day. "Sounds good. Come on in."

"Your sister's so cool," Betsy remarked and Abby nodded. I thought so, too, but was happy they approved.

"Yeah, she's great. It's hard on her with Glen so far away. In the line of fire and all that. But I never lived with my brother or sisters very much before now. This is way cool."

"Well, that's nice. My sister is a real pain in the behind." That topic exhausted, Abby took charge of something else. "I have found the perfect man to take you to homecoming."

I just stared at her. Homecoming wasn't for six weeks, and I was going anyway with or without a date.

"He's the exchange student from Belgium." Abby looked proud, like she'd sculpted him herself or something. "He's like a surfer with an accent. Blond, buff, gorgeous. Touch of 'tude."

I knew who she meant. Gilles van Nullens was all of that, and way out of my league. "Well, what makes you think he'd even ask me?"

"Oh, my angel, if he doesn't, you're going to do the asking. He'll roll panting at your feet."

I was sort of happy with her lopsided compliment, but I took her words as another of her rants. She'd be onto something else inside of a minute.

Instead, I asked about homework. That was more pressing a need than a homecoming date. "What's due? I missed all of Friday, and now most of today."

Abby shrugged as if schoolwork had little importance, and in her case, it really didn't.

"Don't worry about it. Teachers always give you time to make up work," Betsy told me.

"Don't worry about it!" I repeated in disbelief, almost having my fill of both of them. "Of course I worry about it. I'm on scholarship there, you idiots. My schoolwork is very important to me." I felt a little embarrassed, though, having totally forgotten the Salem assignment. Even if everybody has a bad day once in a while, I couldn't afford another one any time soon.

"Well." Betsy clicked her tongue, reached into her purse, and retrieved a folded mess. "We're supposed to think about some project for American Lit. About the Puritans. Mr. Gallindo brought in some examples from past classes. He made a few copies of this one, and I picked it up." She handed me the grubby paper.

"Don't give that scholarship a thought, Delli," Abby declared. "Daddy can fix anything. In fact, he's already called Scat about Ms. Lipsett."

Even Betsy stiffened a bit now.

"Aw, Abby, can't you let it go?" I shook my head and the braid flopped around. "It really isn't any of our business what she does during non-school hours. Maybe she just needs to make ends meet."

Despite its massive tuition, I doubted St. Bart's passed on the profit to teacher salaries.

"That's not the point." Abby's nose lifted high in the air in a familiar way.

Then Betsy and I looked each other in the eyes and nodded together. Like we were hit by the same thunderbolt at the same time.

"Hmmm. Bets, wanna bet a million dollars Ms. Lipsett gave Abby a lousy grade?"

Betsy threw me a thumbs-up.

"Well, Ms. Lipsett aside" — Abby changed subjects again so no one could probe further about her grades — "you should at least go after the cafeteria staff. You got food poisoning!"

"What are you talking about?" I watched, somewhat irritated as Betsy's head this time nodded in rhythm with Abby's. It's like the thunderbolt switched jolts back and forth.

"That tomato juice. Obviously that's what made you sick."

But it wasn't. *God will give you blood to drink.*

"You losers are nuts!" I burst out. "It was the heat and all the running *I* did during P.E. While you stood around like queen bees. Besides" — I pointed at Betsy — "you had some, too."

"Nah-uh. After you started puking, I dumped mine out."

Before Abby could start another tirade, I needed some fresh air for real. A walk through the groves would be just the thing.

"Hey, guys, thanks for stopping by." I did mean it, but I was awfully tired of them. "I wanna get some air. You can take a walk with me or not. I won't get tweaked either way."

"Nah. But thanks for the doughnuts."

"Thanks for the flowers."

After they shut the door, I undid the braid.

~AΩ~

The late afternoon was very hot. The wind had really died down, but it still managed to toss my dad's long gray ponytail across his back. It actually looked like a snake twitching around his shoulders. He was leaning against the wall of the tool shed, observing the Hass avocado trees that grew terraced all over the hill. Our place truly is lovely. Abby and Betsy both called out "Hey Chris!" as they roared out of the driveway in Abby's three-series BMW. I went to him and put my hand in his.

"How's it going?"

"Ah, Delli-dolly." He squeezed my fingers. "Lost some branches. Had some skin damage, but all in all, I think we're going to be OK."

I knew what he meant. It wasn't too bad if only the top layer of an avocado was bruised. The skin is thick and heals quick. But tears in the fruit heal into a callus, and besides being ugly, the fruit doesn't grow evenly. I remembered what Abby said. Chop down those babies, get that ocean view happening, cram the acres with fancy condominiums— which took a lot less land than houses with yards, and my dad probably *was* sitting on a gold mine.

"Just another autumn in southern California." His smile split his face. "The Lord never sends us more than we can bear. And we've been mighty blessed."

"I know." This was definitely a father-daughter moment so calling him "Chris" was out. "Wanna go

46

for a walk with me? I need some air."

He looked embarrassed for a minute, like he'd forgotten why I needed some air. Then he hugged me, worried. "You feeling better? You haven't gotten sick at school since you were about six."

I nodded before the words could start up in my head. "It was just the weather. I sort of overdid it in P.E."

"Well, the winds will stop soon. They don't last much past three days." His gaze turned to sweep the grove. "Then the weather will cool down. Maybe we'll get some rain."

But maybe we wouldn't. Maybe the winds would come back next week even worse. Maybe Dad needed a reminder that he had other options. God did provide, but He also gave us brains to figure out other opportunities. Especially when you least expected them.

"Hey, Dad, do you ever think about selling the grove? You could probably carve up lots to sell but still keep the house." My feet rustled against the gravel because I probably should have kept my mouth shut. Chris is a smart man without me sticking my nose in.

He stopped smiling and sort of glared at me. Right then, I knew for sure that selling wasn't an alternative he'd ever choose.

"Never, dolly. Never. I spent summers here when I was a kid. Never appreciated it. It was like not seeing the forest for the trees." He chuckled at his dumb joke.

"All those years Iris—your mom—and I spent in the Peace Corp and teaching ESL everywhere. Well, it took Uncle Ted dying to make me realize I needed some roots. I'm stayin' for the duration."

Deep down, that's what I wanted to hear. "Take a

walk?" I invited.

"No, doll, but thanks. Hank and I did all the walking around we want to do today."

I gave his cheek a kiss for good luck and set off down a little pathway, some of which was old cement stairs.

Soon the stairs gave way to a gravelly trail that led down the little hill. I could see tons of debris and a lot of windfall fruit, but to me it didn't look worse than other times we'd had storms. And it probably didn't matter. Like my dad, I knew God always does provide. When Dad wanted a career change and good roots, we got led here. Not that it was a good thing, Uncle Ted dying, but then, he'd lived a good life and died in the Lord.

All of a sudden, I had a flashback of the dream. Deliverance walking through the swampy forest of...what was his name? Goodman Crowninshield. What kind of name was that? Maybe if Abby and Betsy hadn't woken me from the dream, Deliverance would have met up with the faceless man again.

What's with that? Recalling the nightmare face made me shudder even in the hot air. I for one didn't want to see *that* again. Deliverance was all on her own there.

Then I saw him.

My own stranger. In my own time.

He stood at the bottom of the hill, near the chain link fence that bordered the road below. His black-booted foot rested on a stump. His fingers were long and elegant, and he held onto a guitar.

"Who are you?" I managed to ask. My heart was beating fast again, but I was more startled than afraid. Then I wondered if I ought to scream for my dad. It wouldn't take him long to get to me. This was definitely private property. The stranger might not be a hit man or anything—he looked like a teenager—but he was a trespasser.

"Sorry," he said, low. "I live up the road. Two-twelve."

He was reciting the address of a house that had been empty for years. The place was such a mess that we neighbor kids declared it haunted.

"The old Lynch place? I didn't know it was for sale." I had to decide. Should I go back up the path to my dad or keep walking toward the stranger? The dream-Deliverance sort of made up my mind for me.

I reached him almost like I couldn't help myself. He began to talk again, and I was glad. Suddenly I was wordless at how beautiful he was. Guys weren't supposed to be beautiful. Handsome. Hot. But not beautiful. Could this day get any weirder?

"Yeah, my dad just bought it. He loves to rehab old places. The worse shape, the better. I'm Gabriel."

Like the archangel. Or like the devil, who was never more real than when he appeared as an angel of light.

Where had *that* come from? My skin suddenly tightened over my bones, and I turned to leave. I couldn't think straight.

"Oh, please don't go. I'm Gabriel Wincott. Call me Gabe."

Hmm. I thought hard. After all, Deliverance hadn't trusted her stranger. But maybe if she had, she wouldn't be alone in the dream now.

"I'm a good guy!" His smile pleaded with me.

"OK." I sighed, "I'm Delli Willis. This is my family's grove."

"Yeah, I met your dad already. He told me to take a look around whenever I want to." He opened his mouth quick, like he wanted to tell me more. But shut it just as fast.

"That's cool," I told him. I was relieved my dad knew him. It made our meeting a little more normal. "It's not that exciting really, but I loved playing in the trees when I was a kid." Then I shut my eyes. I was sounding like I thought *he* was a kid. He had to be seventeen at least.

Then his eyelids stayed closed a second too long like he was thinking hard about what to say next. That got me more than just a little curious.

"What is it? Come on, you can trust me!" I gave him a smile that I hoped was a little bit flirty. It isn't every day that I find out I have a hot neighbor. Well, beautiful.

Even if he was way too pale and way too thin. Now I could see that his blue shirt and black pants hung loose, and not in the baggy style of buying them too large on purpose. The seams met in the right places; just not enough body filled the inside. And although I tried not to stare, I could see that the right side of his face sort of sagged. Like just half of him was tired or something.

He didn't seem to mind my staring, like he might be used to it. Holding the guitar by its neck, he ran his other hand through his tangle of long black hair. It was wavy and not nearly as long as the man's in the swamp. For some reason, I recognized that no stranger entering my life would be blond.

"Well, all right. Since we're neighbors. I'll tell you my deep dark secret." His voice was still low, a little mysterious.

"'Deep, dark secret.' This sounds way too good to miss." I tried to smile, but he was so serious, so mysterious I started to wonder if I should feel nervous or afraid. Maybe I ought to yell for my dad.

But maybe it was a secret that hurt him and made him feel pain. Maybe he just needed a friend. For a second, I felt bad. I didn't really live a very traditional life, but nothing had ever hurt me.

"Here." He gestured for me to sit on the stump while he set himself down in a cushion of leaves. "Well, it's not a bad secret. I just don't tell anyone."

"Then why me?" I asked, looking at his face but he kept his eyes down.

"We're neighbors. Maybe we can be friends."

"Yeah. Maybe." The idea had possibilities. I'd never had a neighbor my own age before. "Are you a musician?" I pointed to the guitar.

His face turned a little red. "No, not much of one at least. The guitar's mostly for therapy. To help me regain the full use of my hands. Well, the right one anyway. The left one's always been OK, which is good since I'm left-handed."

Then he was silent for a long time. I stayed silent, too. If he didn't want to say any more about his big bad secret, I wasn't going to be nosy.

"I've been pretty sick," he said finally, "and I still have a ways to go. But they say I should make a full recovery."

"Wow, Gabe, I'm so sorry." My world had about collapsed just because I'd barfed over some tomato juice. This must be why he was so thin and pale. Interestingly so, by the way. A flash of the Belgian Gilles in his blond beauty and 'tude sparkled in my memory. I didn't understand why, but I realized I liked this tall, thin dark-haired stranger better even though I'd only known him for a few minutes.

"A brain disorder. Pretty rare. It's called AVM. Arteriovenous malformation." He looked off into the trees for a few seconds. "Then I had bleeding on the brain and sort of stroked out during the operation."

My mouth opened, but shock and hot air rushing in wouldn't let me speak. My hand flapped toward him like a broken bird wing.

"It's OK. I still need physical therapy, but I'm walking all right now. Going up and down stairs and hills is good for me." He nudged something with his booted toe, a walking stick to lean on. "And it's blurry, but I should get complete vision back in my right eye soon."

For a weird second, I remembered the blind eyeless hole of Deliverance's stranger. I tried to keep my skin from feeling like I was wearing the itchy wool Mattie spun herself. If I'd met Gabriel first, my dream might make more sense. Things seemed to be going in reverse.

"Man, Gabe. Wow." I felt stupid with my monosyllables, but I couldn't think of anything real to say. He seemed to be finished, but I didn't really want to go. Unlike Deliverance, I wasn't afraid of the devil chasing me, and I wasn't needed at home. I had no need or desire to run away.

Finally, I used real words. "I hope you're all well soon, too, Gabe. Why did you tell me this just now?"

"So you aren't afraid of me."

"Why would I be afraid?"

"A lot of people are." His voice was quiet and gentle. "You'd be surprised. I guess it's because most kids are healthy. They see fine. They don't need a walking stick. If you're thin and sickly, people imagine the worst."

I nodded, figuring what he meant. "Cancer. Chemo."

"Well, sometimes, even worse. AIDS. And like if you touch someone with it, you'll die."

"Yeah, I get it." I did, too. It never was a good thing to be different. At least my friends thought my parents were cool, or I'd be such an outcast. "Well, Gabe, I'm not afraid. Honest. Why don't you play me a song?"

"OK. You asked for it. The only thing I know by heart." He plucked nine deliberate notes.

La-a-a. La-a. La. La. La-a. La. La. La-a. La-a-a.

The nine notes I'd heard before in a dark wood near Salem Village.

"What is that song?" I interrupted him before he could pay anymore. I was terrified. And I was afraid of him. It had nothing to do with his illness. It had everything to do with my dream. But I kept cool. I needed to know the name of the song.

He shrugged. "Some Scottish folk tune. From an old movie my dad likes. *Killiecrankie.*"

I lost air again and couldn't speak the word. Goosebumps crawled up and down my spine like that snake of my dad's hair. Like that morning, queasiness pummeled my gut. I'd been named from something in that movie. Some leader whose regiment called him the Deliverance of the Highlanders. My folks felt the flick had "social relevance" even though the events took place centuries ago. They loved the word, made it my name. I've always been Delli, though, never Deliverance. Even if Delli makes me sound like a kind of restaurant.

"Wanna hear the rest?" he asked.

I shook my head, caught my breath, and forced myself to speak. I could hold off throwing up doughnuts until I got home. "Thanks, but not today. I missed school, and I have some make-up work to do."

"Where do you go to school?"

"St. Bartholomew the Great. St. Bart's for short." I really needed some alone time. "Maybe we can shoot the breeze again sometime."

He laughed as he began to strum again. "Sure. It's not like I don't know where to find you!"

Then he stopped playing and held out a hand.

I ignored him, just in case he wanted to kiss my wrist.

What if he was threatening to stalk me or something?

My dad was no longer standing by the shed, which was good. I knew I looked like the devil was after me as I ran up the back porch steps.

Inside the kitchen, I scrounged for some bread and cheese. Mattie makes bread fresh every day, and it's always like eating a cloud. My mom even grows some of her own grains and has her own special ways of keeping everything fresh, being that she hates chemical preservatives and anything made of plastic.

Aw, she's different but great at the same time. But that's all I needed, right? Something in my stomach besides a sugary doughnut. Maybe Mattie was right, her tirades against sugar. I had to hold back a wild giggle.

What in the world had happened in the grove?

I grabbed some food and collapsed at the kitchen table, which was old and Formica and leftover from Uncle Ted and Auntie Jeanette. As I chewed, I tried to settle down. Nothing had happened. Absolutely nothing. I had met a new neighbor, that's all. Everything else was just coincidence.

That's all. Mere coincidence. I'd never seen the movie *Killiecrankie*, but obviously, I'd heard that song sometime in my life. It was still lurking in my subconscious. Maybe it was a TV commercial jingle or something.

The kitchen was so normal it calmed me right down. Something was gurgling on the stove, so I got up to check it out. If necessary, I could claim to still be sick at dinnertime, if my mom was cooking taro root or parsnips with leeks or any of her other favorites.

But it was just broccoli letting off steam. A platter of salmon stuffed with couscous waited for the oven. That in itself was comforting, and I relaxed. It sure beat Mattie's usual version of seafood, a fish-shaped mound of tofu sprinkled with homegrown dill.

Yeah, life was suddenly normal. I might as well start on homework. That handout Betsy had given me would take all of thirty seconds to read. Since we had to do a project, I already had an idea cooking. A scarlet dress with lace. I could use it for class then wear it to the homecoming dance. Mattie had a relic of a sewing machine and had taught me long ago.

I grabbed a banana to top off the bread and cheese and ran up to my room, which was still pretty hot, but I didn't need any more fresh air today. I knew from the physics syllabus to expect a quiz, which was easy. Betsy's paper had blown onto the floor. I lounged on the bed, getting ready to speed-read.

Some student from the past had concocted a little newsletter-type deal for Mr. Gallindo's project. It was pretty clever, actually. He or she had used facts learned in the witch trial study unit and called it *The Salem Daily News,* dated October 15, 1692. It had want-ads selling flax and lamp oil, and the time of the next religious meeting featuring Cotton Mather. That name sounded familiar. Mr. Gallindo had probably mentioned it.

The backside featured the menu for someplace called Ingersoll's Ordinary. In parenthesis, it read "tavern." Yummy things like Dark Bread, Baked Beans, Pease Porridge, Boiled Meat. And a list of the condemned witches executed in Salem in that awful year.

Well, I found myself spending a lot more than thirty seconds on the assignment, and not speed-reading at all. The list of accused witches ran chronologically, and I read it carefully, passing names of people I knew.

Remembered, I corrected myself. Names *Deliverance* knew.

The tavern owner, whose name was Bridget Bishop. The slattern who had died with a curse on her lips, Sarah Good. Yes, there was Rebecca Nurse. Procter...no, not Elizabeth but John.

A whole passel of them killed on September 22. Tomorrow. That was kind of creepy.

And the last one, hanged on September 24. All alone.

Deliverance Wyllys.

6

It was like seeing your own tombstone. From first grade, maybe even sooner, I knew all about the letter Y meaning the same thing as the letter *I*. Wyllys. Willis. Same difference.

Up to now, I hadn't considered the dream-Deliverance's surname. Was my Deliverance one and the same with the name on the list?

My stomach twisted again, but I kept the bread and cheese down. I couldn't go on throwing up my life. I'd force myself to eat dinner, too, even though it had actually looked good which meant Angie was cooking.

If for one second, Mattie thought I was still sick, I'd have to stay home from school tomorrow, too. I'd miss talking to Mr. Gallindo.

I needed to know who wrote the newsletter. *Maybe it was somebody threatening me.* Once again, my skin felt like it did whenever Mattie knitted me a sweater out of wool sheared and handspun from her three sheep. Hot and itchy like bugs crawling around on me.

But I settled my stomach and my mind. I thought the whole thing through. It was just coincidence. After all, Willis wasn't an unusual name. And no one on earth, except for family, knows me as anything but Delli.

I've never even told Abby and Betsy that stupid Deliverance stuff.

That's it. I felt better. I really did. Now I wouldn't have to get dosed with Mattie's version of Pepto Bismol—goldenrod steeped in barley water. Enough on its own to keep you barfing.

Anyway, Deliverance was probably a real Puritan name. It sounded old fashioned enough, naming a kid after a noun. Like Patience. The dream-Deliverance had a sister that name.

I did, too, come to think of it. And re-enacting the dream once more, hadn't Deliverance's mom mentioned a dead son named Welcome? My heartbeat started its amazing race. My brother Will was Welcome, too.

But then, I got reasonable. All this made even more sense. My dream was just using names and siblings I already had. Probably if I could dream long enough, I'd meet a Peony and Anguish too. (Mattie had had a long labor delivering Angie.)

Coincidence. That's all. Oops. Deliverance's brother William had had a twin named Anguish...

Only one Peony to go. At least my brother and Angie were not twins.

Still, I was a little nervous. The day had been a weird one all around. Maybe Gabe was still exercising his fingers in the grove. He'd confided his big secret with me. I had a feeling he'd understand me. I needed to talk about this to someone objective. Someone with his own unusual situation.

I ran outside and down through the orchard.

"Gabe? Gabriel?" For some reason, I felt like the only person in the world. All I saw were acres of trees, fallen leaves, a few avocados tossed on the ground like big green eggs. Chris and Hank would have already retrieved the good ones, which would ripen later.

But Gabe was gone. I was disappointed. I found the stump where I'd sat a little while ago. I couldn't see any footprints in the leaves and sticks, or even the spot where he had been. It was like he'd never been here. But then, the breeze was brisk, making new piles everywhere, covering up old stuff.

I sat back on the stump, wishing I'd asked Gabe for his phone number. Even if the icky old Lynch house didn't have phones installed yet, he might have his own cell phone like every other kid I know. Mattie and Chris even got me one, for emergencies. Not a fashion accessory. Through babysitting and tutoring at the middle school, I earned just about enough money to pay for it.

Well, I could always walk up the road to Gabe's house, but it was still so hot and I was still so shaky. I sighed and stuck my chin in my hands, elbows on my thighs, deciding what to do next.

Just then, a beautiful yellow bird flitted between two of the trees and perched on a branch ten feet from me. I wanted to reach out my finger, see if it would land on my hand. But I stopped. If I moved, the pretty thing would be scared off.

It was probably waiting for me to leave so it could chow down on a fallen avocado or something. It looked straight at me, its bright little eyes like black beads.

I didn't want to disturb the bird. As quiet as I could, I started back to the house. My dad was waiting at the top of the path.

"You OK, honey? Did I hear you calling someone?"

I smiled back at his sweet concern. He was way different from most dads around here. Dads like

Abby's who had lots of money and wore designer suits and drove cars that cost more than my dad made in a year. Oakton is a pretty expensive Southern California enclave with secluded homes and groves and ranches surrounded by lots of private woodsy hills. Without Uncle Ted, there was no way the Willises would be living in an area like this.

"Yeah, I'm fine, Dad." I felt more and more comfortable calling him Dad instead of his first name. It just sounded more normal, more like a daughter. "I just met that guy from the old Lynch place and forgot to ask him something."

"I think I saw him go back up the hill a few minutes ago," my dad said. "Seems like a nice kid. Sorry you missed him. It'll be good to have some neighbors up close again."

"Yeah, I think it will be nice. How come nobody's ever lived there?" I knew the neighbors down the hill, of course, the Jumpers and the Edwardses, but they were acres away, too.

"No big mystery, really. I remember the Lynches from long ago. They never had any kids. When the mister died, the missus moved to Florida or somewhere and couldn't bear to part with the place. I guess she passed on last year, and her heirs decided to sell."

We walked back up toward the house. I shrugged kind of disappointed. That was pretty boring. A mystery, like a double murder or something, would have been so much cooler. The Lynch house was supposed to be haunted. I remembered something else interesting that would make my dad happy. He liked nature, hiking, and animals much better than old houses. "I just saw the most amazing bird."

My dad's eyes lit up.

"A pretty yellow bird," I pointed down the hill, "Just sat on a branch flirting with me."

"A goldfinch maybe. Did it have some black feathers, too?" He smiled. "I haven't seen one around here for a long time."

I shrugged. "No. Just yellow and like I said, very pretty."

His ponytail wiggled as he shrugged back. "Maybe some kind of canary."

"Like a songbird in a cage? On the loose?"

"Nah. Something wild. I don't really know. Let's take it as a good luck charm."

I remembered something not as pleasant. What was it? I thought hard, back to the dream. *Bewitching innocent girls with fortune-telling and conjuring and charms.*

Seeing the Tall Man.

I shivered in spite of the heat. "No, Dad, just a bird. Not a charm or anything."

He looked at me with some surprise. I realized I had used a pretty sharp tone of voice, so I gave him a quick hug of apology.

"Misspoke, dolly girl. I meant sign of goodness, from our Lord."

Of course, it was just a bird. And Gabe couldn't help being awfully tall.

~AΩ~

"Gracey! Stop wiping your mouth with your sleeve! McKenna, you better knock it off and eat your fish."

Angie was obviously in a crummy mood, and I

realized I couldn't confide in her either. It happens sometimes when my sister watches the evening news and learns more about planes like Glen's patrolling the no-fly zone in the Middle East. I couldn't imagine how awful it must be to have the man you love so far away.

I even sort of missed Gabe, and I didn't know him at all, much less love him. It's just that I wanted to have someone to talk to, and I'd decided he wasn't scary.

Just like Deliverance was missing the man in the woods.

Yuck. I shook that thought away as I attacked the salmon, which actually was pretty good. There were many advantages to having Angie living in the house, even if she had bad moods sometimes. She'd been here a month. She could cook and liked doing it.

I felt it only fair to offer to do the dishes, but both Angie and Mattie shooed me off. Cleanup was never all that bad because Great Aunt Jeannette had installed a dishwasher over the years. Amazingly, it still worked. Even still, my mom felt it simplified one's soul to perform everyday tasks without the complications of the modern world. Especially when using her hand-woven linen dishtowels. Luckily, Angie and I did not share this view. I left my sister busily loading the appliance.

Oh, well. They probably just wanted to get rid of me in case I got sick again and tossed up my dinner all over everything. My room was still too hot, so I ended up in my dad's cluttered study.

A while back, he and Mattie had no choice but to allow modern technology into our house to help them run the bookstore and the avocado business. Mattie offers a bit of romance and a few bestsellers and children's books, but also less mainstream inventory:

devotional materials, liturgical art, church histories, obscure folktales, and tracts on esoteric subjects like Christian mysticism and stuff. And of course her hand-stitched journals and her self-published books on cooking and herbal remedies. She also sells her tea towels and handmade jewelry that she consigns from local artisans. It's actually a very beautiful, artful, non-traditional place, just like Mattie.

And she's got a loyal following, serves refreshments to each customer whether they buy anything or not. On Saturdays, she takes reservations for high tea. Dad's computer helps her keep track of buyers, visitors, recipes, and menus.

I know Mattie would prefer using her own handmade paper and natural-dye inks for her accounts, but she has accepted her digital fate. Although making money has never meant much to either of my parents, they know they need to stay in the black for basic survival.

But now I just needed a plain old encyclopedia. My folks had an ancient set from Uncle Ted's day, but I figured the history of Salem hadn't changed. I looked around for the volume I needed and wondered again about the strange dreams and feelings I'd been having. For a second, I even considered that maybe I really was getting some kind of sickness and ought to depend more on Mattie's remedies. Even though they're unusual, they almost always work. I'd prayed a ton during the day whenever I thought about things, so hopefully the Lord would help out, too.

Finally, I found what I was looking for. The last hangings of Salem's witches had been September 22, 1692. That was fact. Nothing had happened two days later. I couldn't help sighing in relief.

Better yet, nobody named Deliverance Wyllys figured into any of it.

Just as I sighed in relief a second time, the telephone rang. It was attached to the fax machine, another Willis concession to modern times, and I picked up the receiver.

"Delli?"

It was Gabe. I could already recognize his voice.

I tried to keep my heart from fluttering a little. That was lame to begin with as well as confusing. I didn't even know him. Besides, he was sickly and strange. And on top of all that, Abby was trying to match make me with Gilles van Nullens, the hottest exchange student ever. Going to the homecoming dance with Gilles would be a real triumph. I'd be in about a million yearbook pictures.

"Delli?" Gabe's voice was excited, almost too loud. I practically had to hold the receiver away from my ear. "I looked up your number. I had to tell you. I'm going to enroll at St. Bart's tomorrow!"

"What? Why? I mean, that's great." And it was, in a way. I'd have heads up on another cool guy joining the ranks. Unless, of course, everybody else managed to conclude he was a dork. The fact that I thought him cool didn't mean a thing of itself. Kids like Abby and Gilles were the ones with clout.

"Yeah. My dad home schooled me while I was recuperating, but he says it's time to get with the program. He's done a lot of research about the local schools. St. Bart's has the best reputation. But most of all, my dad talked to your dad, and he said *you're* really happy there."

I didn't know if Gabe had a mom or why she didn't have a say. This didn't seem the time to ask. If we went to the same school every day, I could find out more about him. And it almost sounded like my being there had something to do with his decision. That was sort of a compliment.

"Well, I think it's been a good decision. I've got some wonderful friends." I tried not to snort, remembering how annoying Abby and Betsy had been today. "The teachers really are great."

Well, some of them at least. I thought of Mr. Gallindo and Coach Clayter. They were all right. But I also thought of Scat—yuck—and Ms. Lipsett whom Abby had declared sleazy.

"Well, most of the teachers, I mean." I nodded even though Gabe couldn't see me. Maybe I should talk to him about Ms. Lipsett and see if her being a barmaid would affect his decision. I had a feeling he'd be honest with me.

"Thing is," Gabe was saying, "I was wondering if you wouldn't mind if I pick you up in the morning."

The idea made me nervous in a good way, almost like it was a date or something. But he was probably just nervous too, starting off at a new school where he didn't know anybody. I'd been awfully scared that first day my freshman year. Abby had introduced herself right away and taken me right under her wing. Now I could do pretty much the same thing with Gabe.

"I'd love to," I told him, feeling dumb because it sounded like I was agreeing to a date. "I can show you where your classes are. Maybe introduce you to the teachers and some of my friends."

"I was sorta hoping that." He sounded shy. "And hey, Delli..."

I already knew what he was going to ask. "You don't have to worry, Gabe. I won't tell anybody about...you know. But..."

Even though there weren't any stairs at St. Bart's, the school buildings were scattered all over a rolling rural campus.

"...you might need your walking stick."

I almost heard him smile over the phone.

"OK," he said. "It's a really cool walking stick. A carved shillelagh from Ireland. More a conversation piece than a crutch."

"That does sound cool. OK, then. We need to leave here about seven thirty." I'd need to get up way early to make sure my hair didn't end up like a Brillo pad.

"I'll be there."

I was somehow excited, maybe because the day had been so strange and this was something new to look forward to. At least no one else at home would have to worry about getting me to school in the morning. I decided to take a long bath and wash the day from my body. Then I could relax in bed with MTV blaring. My mom decried the station as violent and misogynistic, but my dad liked it so that made it OK.

Actually, my mom doesn't think television is necessary at all, but her kids had never really taken this opinion seriously. Fortunately neither does her husband who now even subscribes to cable.

I stepped into the water and yelped. It was almost too hot. But I gritted my teeth and let the water cover every inch of my skin, other than my face of course. Great Aunt Jeanette and Great Uncle Ted had been pretty petite people, but they had picked a bathtub big enough for the Olympic swim team. I breathed deep, the scent of Mattie's homemade bath oils filling my nose.

Mattie's bath oils are one of her strong points, just like the bread she bakes. She sells bath oils at the bookshop in little earthenware bottles she throws on her own potter's wheel and fires in her own kiln behind the sheep shed. She mixes up natural glazes for the pottery too, and concocts handmade soaps. And of course makes the hand-pressed paper and natural-dye inks. Now my mom's lavender and rosemary calmed me down. Mattie grows both those herbs, and a jillion others, in her large garden east of the sheep shed.

The herbs started to relax me. I hoped—*really* hoped—that neither Abby nor Betsy would call. I deserved a long peaceful soak after the day I'd had.

The water was still very hot. Maybe I should get a drink of cool water. I was so very, very hot...

7

"Water! Cool water for my tormented child!"

Goodwife Putnam's voice was much too loud for the hushed courtroom. Her behavior was immodest, but Deliverance could understand the woman's urgent wish to calm the fits of her anguished daughter.

Yet, even as she watched young Ann's convulsions on the floor, Deliverance almost envied the idea of cool water. She was monstrously hot. Although the meetinghouse was intended for worship, today it was once again a courtroom, crowded with townsfolk: witnesses, spectators, citizens accused of witchcraft.

And of course, the afflicted girls who accused them.

The hot, stale air nearly choked her. Deliverance held a little bundle of linen close to her nose. Inside it, she'd stuffed some sprigs of lavender and rosemary from her mother's tiny medicinal garden. The peaceful scents helped ease the body odors clogging her nostrils.

The good folk of Salem were both restless and frightened after another full day of trial. Yet no one dared to leave. Doing so would cause suspicion. No one wanted to draw the attention of the circle of afflicted girls. Their calling out names could remind other people of new evidence that had long been forgotten.

New evidence that could seal the conviction of

someone, who just yesterday had been a respectable farmer or goodwife.

Deliverance shuddered. Ann was her friend, and the strange symptoms frightened her. First, Ann twitched and moaned. Then her bones stiffened most unnaturally, her sinews strung like bowstrings. Mary Warren had told Deliverance in secret that the girls practiced foolery, but how could suffering like this be false?

Suddenly, Ann sat up, eyes wild in new horror.

"She chokes me! She chokes me!" Then she retched and vomited all over herself, in front of everyone she knew.

Added to the steaming foul air, the scent of Ann's bile made Deliverance gag too, in spite of her fragrant bundle. Next to her, her honored mother stiffened at the unpleasantness of the entire scene.

"She chokes me!"

Goody Putnam knelt close to her daughter, as if listening carefully.

"Martha Carrier." Goody Putnam lifted her head to the magistrate high in his seat. "She names Goody Carrier as her tormenter."

The crowd burst out in gasps and shouts. Goody Carrier was already chained to the prison walls for casting a spell that sickened a farmer's cattle.

"Martha Carrier!" Ann yelled again into the air.

"Judge Hathorne, she hath bewitched my cattle as well," shouted out a farmer whom Deliverance had always thought wise and kindly. "'Tis no surprise she's 'witching' innocent children!"

"Hold your tongue, Benjamin Abbot." Another man fumed. "Salem has long known that you dispute the boundaries of my mother's land."

"Silence, Richard Carrier!" ordered the judge.

"But my mother has been jailed these weeks! How can she cause harm to anyone here?"

Before the judge could say another word, Goody Putnam waved her hands at the excited throng. "All here know that a witch's shape can leave her body behind in its search to do evil," she announced. "Indeed, the Reverend Cotton Mather himself declares that one's specter causes as much harm as the fleshly form."

"Aye, true enough," said Judge Hathorne, almost wearily. "Reverend Mather has indeed decreed that spectral evidence may be entered as rightful testimony. 'Tis the sole task of this Court of Oyer and Terminer to root out evil. All evidence must be considered."

Deliverance heard the fancy words and thought them silly. They meant To Hear and Determine. Why not say it as it is?

Then she watched Goody Putnam give Goodman Abbot a quick look. Gratitude shone in Goody's eyes rather than distress at her daughter's torment. Was the woman herself up to mischief as Deliverance's honored mother had suggested? Her skin felt like it did when a new winter chemise touched her body for the first time. When wool scratched rather than warmed.

Suddenly, as they had done at every trial all summer long, the whole passel of Salem's afflicted girls began to thrash about and whimper on the floor as well.

"She pricks me," a girl called out to no one in particular as she shuddered and wiggled. "Goody Carrier pricks me with pins."

The spectators shouted in horror almost as one voice.

"I see Goody Carrier," another girl cried, her arms flailing in a wild upward gesture.

Deliverance knew both girls well. Reverend Parris' daughter and niece. Grabbing her mother's hand, Deliverance and the entire gathering looked toward the ceiling.

"'Tis her shape! I see her! I see Goody Carrier sitting on a beam." The two girls shrieked again. Soon Ann Putnam recovered enough to join in with them.

"I see...another specter. Elizabeth Procter."

The last name had been called out by Mary Warren. Deliverance was staggered. The Procters employed Mary and were good to her. Since she had obviously changed her mind and stayed with the circle girls, maybe they truly were not playacting. Maybe Satan had truly come to Salem.

Deliverance felt ill. *Maybe Satan had truly come to Salem.* Even still, she didn't see any shapes sitting on the beams.

Then one of the Parris girls called out again. "See it? See it flying?" Then all the girls waved their arms dreamily.

Deliverance's skin felt like the inside of her nose did when she breathed frigid air. She knew what the girls meant. She didn't know why, but she almost saw it in her mind.

A yellow bird.

"A yellow bird. Oh see, a yellow bird," shrieked the little Parris girl.

Deliverance's skin grew damp with horror.

"'Tis the devil's *familiar*," Goody Putnam howled. "We good Christians know that a witch cannot speak directly to the devil."

"No bird, not a bird. Not the devil's familiar,"

Reverend Parris' niece started softly, then shouted with rampant terror. "I've see the demon himself."

"What, child?" Her uncle's voice soothed.

"In the marshes. For the past five gloamings. His black hair covers his face like a bat's wing. Like a veil of hell's darkness."

"Child, are you certain?"

Eyes glazed, the girl nodded her head wildly.

"Then he must be captured." Several goodmen announced, tensing with readiness.

The blood in Deliverance's veins stopped running through them. Terror washed over her, a terror even worse than seeing her friends in fits and convulsions before her. A terror worse than knowing once-kindly folk had turned witch.

A terror worse than hearing neighbors cast accusations against their friends, even family, for slights and wrongs never made right.

Shamefully, her terror was for the man in the swamp. A man whose name she didn't even know. A man who played forbidden music and left witch's kisses with his ruined mouth. A man who was too monstrous to live among civilized folk.

A man who might truly be the Tall Man, waiting for the unsuspecting to sign his book. To give him their souls and receive in return the dominions of the earth.

She could barely swallow. Was Goody Carrier choking her as well?

Protect me, Lord.

Secretly, she lifted the cuff of her sleeve so that she could glance at her wrist. The little mark was there but had faded so that it was barely visible. For a strange moment, seeing it gave her comfort. But knowing it was healing made her sad.

He was no demon. She knew that in her heart. But the good folk of Salem would think so if they captured him.

She had to warn him. She had to warn him now! Before the frenzied crowd searched him out.

Just thinking of the dank, dark swamp and his tortured face made her turn colder than she had ever been, colder than a midnight in deep midwinter. Her heart beat faster than it ever had before. Even the night her good father lay dying.

But she had to warn the man in the marsh.

She had to leave now without being noticed. Everyone's attention was on the circle girls, giving her a chance to slip away.

"Mother, I must use the privy," she whispered as she shoved her way outside. In spite of the heat, cold wetness dropped on Deliverance's head, and she felt colder than ever. Was it possible that mighty God in His providence had sent rain to ease the summer's drought? The sky seemed blue, but her wet hair lay like dead snakes across her arms.

~AΩ~

"C-mon, mommy needs to wash us up. Then we get popcorn. You clean enough now."

Gracey stood with the bathroom drinking glass. Bending down, she filled it with my bathwater that had grown cold. Then she poured another cupful over my head.

I was shivering with cold. As I shook away the water drops, I forced myself to wake up. My heart was pounding so hard it hurt.

"Stop it, you brat!" I yelled.

"I'm gonna tell G'amma you call me names," Gracey said, pout lip huge as she ran out of the room.

I barely heard her. Even though I knew I was safe, home, in our own bathroom, I couldn't even move. How on earth could I have fallen asleep in the bathtub? I might have drowned. I thanked God the ancient bathroom door lock usually doesn't work. That's why the Willis family knocks first. That broken lock has too much history for my dad to replace it.

Angie was teaching her girls to knock, but in this case, I didn't really mind Gracey's lack of manners. At least my next bed wouldn't be my coffin.

I thanked God for keeping me safe, too, and finally calmed down. All I'd done was unwind a little bit too much in a hot tub reeking with my mom's relaxing herbs, and I'd had a dream. A stupid dream. I hadn't dreamed this much in years, in my whole life really, but dreams were all they were.

I'd dreamed about a yellow bird because I'd seen one today. And all those Puritan people. Well, I'd just read a bunch of names in that class project newsletter and that encyclopedia.

But deep inside, I had to admit it. I was almost starting to worry about a dream-man in a creepy swamp three hundred years ago. Who wasn't even real. Maybe I ought to ask God to keep me safe some more, although it was *such* a lame reason. I know He knows everything, but even He might not get it. For a funny second, I couldn't help myself and I glanced at my wrist.

My wrist was smooth and unmarked, still tan from summer. It was just a stupid dream, after all.

I dried off, remembering instead the good feelings about going to school with Gabe in the morning.

Something a little different in the grand scheme of my life so far. Then I realized my throat was starting to hurt a little.

No, a lot.

I headed downstairs for one of Mattie's weird but amazing cures. I didn't want to miss school for any reason at all.

And stupidly, I couldn't stop thinking about Deliverance when she wondered if Goody Carrier was choking her as well.

8

At the field, I sat on a bench on the sidelines, watching the rest of the class play speedball in the dewy grass. The bench was maroon and had the school logo painted on it. Scat had insisted on wasting money that way. My mom had sent a note excusing me from dressing out because of my little sore throat, which didn't hurt all that much, but I was glad for some alone time to think things through.

But then Abby started heading toward me, and I clucked in impatience. I didn't care if Abby heard.

"How ya feeling?" Abby spoke first, sincere, then announced cheerfully, "Coach Clayter says I don't have to dress out today. I have cramps."

"You poor thing," I said.

"So tell me *everything*." Abby started out, kind of suggestively, but then she giggled.

"You're in an awfully good mood for a girl who just whined herself out of P.E. because of cramps." I admit I snarked.

That just made Abby laugh louder. I knew perfectly well that nothing was wrong with her. She just wanted to bug me into finding out about Gabe. Obviously, Coach Clayter has wisely decided not to mess with Abby. I wondered if the coach suspected that Abby was behind yesterday's meeting with Scat.

Majorly annoyed, I ached to ignore Abby. I really had wanted some time alone. My throat was better, and I hadn't had a dream all night, but the morning had been weird. I hadn't expected Gabe's *dad* to drive us to school. At St. Bart's, senior boys had their own wheels, and pricey ones at that.

Besides, if I'd known, I might have pretended to be sick and stayed home. In retrospect, his dad driving us was pretty lame.

"You *better* tell me everything!" Abby ordered, although I already decided I wouldn't. She smiled expectantly anyway. "Who's that hot guy you were with this morning? And wow, arriving in a *limo*. My, my."

Hmm. That was a pretty cool way of looking at it. The car *was* an elderly, but absolutely pristine, Rolls Royce. And if everybody thought Gabe had a limo driver, yeah, that could really work toward coolness.

Still I didn't answer. I really shouldn't be peeved at Gabe. I understood. I really did. His vision and reflexes weren't quite where the doctors wanted them to be before he got his driver's license back.

So I decided to remember how good he looked in the St. Bart's uniform. Burgundy polo shirt and khaki slacks. However, it wouldn't be long before Scat made him cut his long hair. Maybe even before tomorrow.

Since I'd had to get a readmit slip and he needed to see the registrar, we'd walked together all the way across campus to the main office. It had been rather fabulous to have the whole student body watching us.

He hadn't had any sort of limp that I could notice and had kind of twirled his walking stick like a baton rather than lean on it. I'm sure it intrigued everybody. Abby had called out to me from the student parking lot, but I hadn't felt like dealing with her just then. Or now, really.

"C'mon, girlfriend!" Abby insisted now, her leg tensing because I knew she really wanted to stamp her foot. "What's up with you and him? Who is he?"

Still not saying anything, I pretended to be interested in the P.E. game for a minute. Betsy was following all the rules, which she always did when Abby wasn't around, but every once in a while she looked longingly over at us.

The morning was lots cooler than yesterday, and the wind had died down. The weather almost felt like fall. Well, as fall as Southern California gets. The hills around us were covered mostly with live oak and avocado groves, but here and there, I could see a tree trying to change color. The area was very pretty. Los Angeles seemed a lot farther than sixty miles away.

I remembered the damp dark swamp and shivered a little, but also remembered how hot Deliverance had been in the stuffy courtroom. Maybe Salem was getting some cool sea breezes today.

Today? My muscles tensed, my skin turned cold. What on earth was happening in my mind? *Today?*

Today was three hundred years later. Besides, Deliverance didn't live in Salem. She lived in a dream. In fact, I'd slept like a baby all night long and hadn't dreamed a single thing. Mattie's bedtime tincture of fig, licorice, and yarrow had worked wonders.

Maybe Deliverance was gone for good, and I was done with all of this.

Maybe Deliverance had been able to warn the disfigured man in the woods.

Or maybe he truly was a demon. Did I even want to know?

"C'mon!" Abby's teeth gritted with impatience, like they always did when she didn't instantly get her way. She plunked herself next to me on the bench. That immediately let me know I was back in my normal world again. "C'mon, Del-woman, this isn't funny anymore. Who is he, and what on earth is he doing with *you*?"

Abby actually sounded insulting with that remark, but I didn't let it rile me. Abby didn't mean anything. She just had so much on her mind with her messed up family. Besides, I just wanted to feel good, happy. I'd prayed for peace before going to bed, and it looked like the Lord had listened.

Plus my day had gotten off to a good start. I was feeling pretty well, and my hair had behaved perfectly for once. Mr. Wincott had stopped at the Cruller, and Gabe had bought me a cappuccino to thank me for going with him.

Besides, I confess to wanting to stretch out the secret as long as I could. Never before had I had any kind of upper hand with Abby. It some sick way, this felt good, too. I probably ought to repent, but it just wouldn't be now.

"Forget it then." Abby grumbled in a way I knew well but never alarmed me. "He's probably gay or something. That walking stick was pretty lame."

That got me to react. Spreading nonsense like that was just something Abby might try if something got in her way.

"Oh, for crying out loud, can't you ever stop being a spoiled princess?" My good mood had practically vanished. Mrs. Goodman abandoning her family was awful, but shouldn't Abby be trying to deal with it? She wasn't two years old. Mrs. Mergen is a great counselor, and so is my pastor.

"You're the spoiled princess, not letting me meet

him!" Abby pouted. "I called out to you and you just kept on walking."

Well, Abby was right about all of that, but I refused to feel guilty. Although I decided to relent. I didn't know how it felt to have your family implode, and I did have sympathy for Abby. Besides, she and Gabe were both my friends. Sooner or later, they'd need to meet and be friends, too.

"OK, I'll introduce you after school. Personally I think the walking stick is kinda jaunty."

"Well, I do, too." Abby smiled in agreement for a second before her eyes narrowed in a sort of suspicion. "Where'd he come from? Is he related to Angie?"

It was almost like I needed her approval or something.

"Well, if he's related to Angie, he's also related to me," I said, "considering that we're sisters."

Betsy actually scored a goal right then, and I stood up and cheered.

Abby joined me, blushing a little. "I meant, maybe he's related to her through her husband or something," she asked after we got quiet again.

That actually sounded reasonable, so I started to yield.

"No relation. We just met yesterday."

"When? I thought you were home sick."

"Well, in the afternoon."

"Bets and I were with you then."

"Not all day," I reminded her. "After you left, I walked through our orchard for some fresh air. He was…there." I didn't mention the guitar. Gabe was expecting me to keep his secret, and I wasn't sure what all he wanted to reveal.

"Why?"

I really did understand Abby's wild curiosity. Girls met cute guys at the beach or the mall, not in a dark grove.

Or a dark swamp. I got rid of that thought quick, though. Deliverance's swamp-man wasn't all that cute. Well, half of him anyway.

"He's a senior. They just moved here. His dad bought the old Lynch place and is going to fix it up." I smiled and stretched, figuring it was going to be a good day.

Hearing that, Abby turned hostile. "The old Lynch place? My dad's had a standing offer for that property for years and years!"

I shrugged. Some of my parents' disinterest in material goods had rubbed off. "Well, I can't answer to that. Maybe his dad paid more or something."

"I doubt it." Abby was clearly angry. Tension all but rippled her skin. "That's totally bogus. My dad's got his heart set on developing Skyline Lane."

"What do you mean?" I also tensed up. I had some suspicions of my own now, considering that was the street where we lived, too.

"I mean, there's no way he wants that trashy old Lynch dump." Her bottom lip stuck out so far she might have gotten a collagen implant before school. "He plans to put in million-dollar estates. He wants to tear the house down and clear off the lot and fit in a dozen of them. Your place, too, if your dad would agree to sell. I mean, believe me. Daddy's willing to pay a *ton*."

I knew that and had even just yesterday asked my dad if he thought he ought to sell. But he didn't want to, and I was glad. But Abby loved her dad like I loved mine, so I tried to calm her down. "You know, Abs, I don't think you can just carve up a hillside." I wasn't being argumentative, honest. "Some of those oak trees are protected by law. There're always rules and zoning laws. All of that stuff."

"You don't think *my dad* knows about zoning?" Abby's tongue clicked against her teeth almost like she wore a tongue ring. "He's a real estate developer, for heaven's sake, and he's got a legal staff as big as your family. He wouldn't want to buy land he couldn't build on! Ah man, he's totally going to freak." She stuck her legs straight out in front of her, tight as a rubber band ready to fire. "He's gonna totally *freak*."

She looked straight into my eyes then. "I might have to do something about it."

The morning sun had grown a lot warmer, but hearing Abby, I felt that same midnight chill I'd felt in the courtroom.

I mean the chill that *Deliverance* had felt. Unseen fingers tickled my spine, and I prayed for quick calm.

But that was then. This was now. I took a deep breath. "What are you talking about, Abby? You mean, like getting Coach Clayter in trouble? Or getting Ms. Lipsett fired?"

"No." The fire went out of Abby's voice. "Coach is OK. She was cool about me having cramps today, but I think Daddy's still concerned about Ms. Lipsett. What I meant now is that we're going to have to convince him—what's his name—"

"Gabe Wincott."

"We're going to have to convince Gabe Wincott to work on his dad to sell it at a huge profit. I mean, before he starts putting money into the remodeling and everything. Why waste the money? Daddy will pay anything they ask."

I rolled my eyes, surprised my sockets ached. Maybe I hadn't slept as well as I thought. "Abby, just forget it. There's no 'we' in any of this. That's what Mr. Wincott does. Rebuilds trashed old houses. Your dad builds new ones. He has other land where he can do it, but beat-up old houses, well, they're in shorter supply."

Abby twirled her feet angrily. "Skyline Lane is important to my dad, Delli. I can't explain it. He's got a vision, and his visions are always right. But…"

"But what…?"

"It's more than that. Ever since my mom left him…left us, he's just not focused. It would be so good for him. To have something go right. I just want to make him happy."

As bad as I felt about Abby's mom running off, I just couldn't think that the well-being of Abby's dad depended on evicting another family from its dream.

"Oh, Abby, let it go." I tried to be firm. "Your dad's business dealings have nothing to do with you. He's already very successful. I'm sure he's got other developments going on."

"Delli!" My name came out from those gritted teeth.

"Have a good day, Abs."

By this time, Coach Clayter was yelling at the class to shower and change. Since I didn't have to do either, I started out early for the American Lit classroom. That way I'd have a few minutes to talk to Mr. Gallindo about that 1692 newsletter before class started.

I just needed to make sure that the newsletter wasn't some sort of threat. People were so weird and mean. Just listen to Abby. Even if she did have an excuse.

~AΩ~

Gabe waved to me when I passed him in the small hall. He leaned on his walking stick, chatting with some other seniors. Including a nominee for homecoming queen. A funny little jealousy rippled across my skin, but I shook it off. Of course, Gabe would be making new friends, lots of them. And some would be girls. He looked happy and healthy and that was all that mattered.

Besides, Mattie had raised me to know that my happiness—my life—depended only on me. Not some guy. Which I thought was cute and funny coming from her. Not that I don't accept or believe her. I do. It's just that she and my dad have been totally together since they were like thirteen. Then again, Mattie promised that God had a plan for me, me alone, and while she hoped I found true love someday like she did, I was special to Him all on my own.

Mr. Gallindo sat at his desk, skimming a handful of papers.

"Mr. G., are you busy?"

He probably was—class was starting in a couple of minutes—but he motioned me inside. "Feeling better?"

I nodded but didn't explain anything. St. Bart's was a small campus, and Mr. Gallindo was the sort of teacher who knew everything anyway. That's one reason I wanted to talk to him.

And probably the reason Scat wanted to get rid of him.

"Sure you're not busy?"

"I'm just reviewing my notes for today's lecture, but I'm almost done." His wrinkly eyes twinkled at me. "What can I do you for?"

I knew he was trying to be funny, saying that instead of "what can I do for you?" but I was more surprised that he was doing some studying himself. Since he'd been teaching American Lit for a gazillion years, I'd just figured he knew everything he needed to know. I told him so.

"Not on your life, kiddo. The day I stop learning is the day I die."

Hmm. That was kind of a cool attitude. Truth was, he sounded a lot like Chris and Mattie, and I had to smile. "I was just wondering, Mr. Gallindo, if…well, if you know how many people died in Salem? The witch trials I mean."

"Twenty."

I breathed the same sigh of relief as last night. Still…

"Positive?" I tried to laugh.

"Positutely and *absotively*." He grinned at his own silly cleverness. "The Puritans were highly educated and kept remarkable records. Entirely subjective, propaganda-style records." He grinned again, but a bit sour. "But facts like names and dates have never been disputed."

He was just verifying what I'd learned last night, but I had to see what he thought about the fictional victim whose name was so like mine.

I dug around in the bottom of my backpack for the little Salem newsletter and groaned. It had somehow slipped out of my folder and now was a crumpled mess, like a piece of trash. I smoothed it as best I could.

Bad luck.

"Betsy brought me this yesterday and told me about the project. I'm wondering if you might remember who did this?"

He peered at it over his glasses. "Not off hand. I see a hundred projects every year. This is a photocopy of the original and looks like I blanked out the student's name first before using this as an example. Let me see if I still have the original." He got up and rummaged in a storage cupboard.

"Sorry, seems I don't have my finger on the original right now, Del. Those photocopies were left over from another semester. Is it important?"

It kind of was, therefore I didn't remind him that nobody called me Del. But when I scanned down the list of names to show him the name so much like mine, it was just a smudgy rip. I didn't understand; I'd put the thing carefully in a manila file folder. It was almost like an unseen hand had pulled it out to mess with it.

Or more logically, Gracey or McKenna had gotten into my stuff before I left this morning. Even if they had been still asleep when Mr. Wincott picked me up.

No way could I try to explain this one. The unseen hand tickled my spine, and I cleared my throat so my voice wouldn't shake. "No, I just wondered if I…could borrow the same sort of idea."

Big grin again. "Sure. That's why I show examples of past projects. Just be sure, of course, to make sure your content and design are completely your own."

I was a little disappointed but a lot relieved. Deliverance hadn't died in Salem after all. The old-time version of her name was just some other student's original "design and content." Just then, a noisy jock called out, "Hey, Mr. G., what we gonna learn today?"

Without meaning to, I spoke the words out loud with Mr. Gallindo as he answered.

"The Trial of Martha Carrier."

Mr. Gallindo laughed out loud even with the surprise on his face. "You getting psychic on me, Willis?" Obviously, he'd recalled my feelings about Del.

I had to say something, anything. He'd think I was taking drugs, or worse, he'd drag me to the school counselor again. So I shrugged.

"Lucky guess. I looked ahead in the textbook." I hadn't of course, and I felt bad about lying, shot up a quick request for forgiveness, but he wouldn't let it go.

"You do seem to know a lot more than average about Salem."

Well, he was right, but I wasn't about to explain why. I'd earned enough brownnoser points yesterday. That was good enough. "Yeah," was all I said.

"Well, I'm sure your mother's mentioned the subject over the years," Mr. Gallindo explained knowingly. "She always carries interesting topics in her shop."

I nodded, actually feeling comforted. He was probably right.

The jock whose real name was Josh Taggart wasn't done learning yet. "I don't get these Puritans, though, Mr. G. I mean, didn't they start Harvard and all? How could they believe all this witch bull?"

Mr. G. had us all enthralled even before the bell rang. For the first time, my desk actually felt like a place I wanted to be for a while. Josh slouched down, and I could easily see over him.

"Even among educated, religious people in the seventeenth century, witchcraft was real." Mr. Gallindo perched on the edge of his desk and spoke to the class like he was holding a conversation, not lecturing. "After all, folks needed explanations for the events of their lives. Remember, this all happened before the Age of Reason and scientific theories."

"Huh?" This was Josh's standard response in any occasion.

"Let's see. OK, you're a God-fearing farmer and a cow falls sick." After Josh nodded, Mr. Gallindo went on. "You don't know anything about bacteria or viruses. Then another cow, and another dies. Soon you've lost your entire herd. All this time you've been having arguments with a grumpy neighbor. So it makes perfect sense to believe that the neighbor cast a spell on your cows."

"But those girls...?"

"...didn't want to get into trouble for listening to a slave woman from Barbados. They were bored during a long winter and Tituba's tales of curses and conjuring thrilled them. But such topics were literally against the law. The girls needed an excuse for behaving so inappropriately. So, of course, the grownups blamed Tituba for bewitching their little daughters. That's when the girls realized their power. They literally were given permission to 'find witches.' It became easy then to use this power to take revenge."

"But weren't witches burned at the stake?" Betsy asked now.

Mr. Gallindo shook his head. "In Catholic countries, witchcraft was considered heresy, and the penalty was burning. Britain and its colonies, being Protestant, considered the offense a felony, and the punishment therefore was hanging."

I listened pretty intently for a while. Mr. Gallindo was very knowledgeable, very enthused, and Josh Taggart started asking some intelligent questions. My skin turned both hot and cold, like it had in the bath last night, when "Mr. G." talked about Martha Carrier's trial. When he mentioned the names of some of her accusers, I realized they were people I'd dreamed about.

But freaked as I was, I wasn't about to run scared and screaming, blaming somebody else for something I couldn't understand. Not like those wackos in Salem.

I'd figure it all out, maybe with the help of some friends. Spend a lot longer in prayer tonight than the quick "Now I Lay Me" from childhood. Not that I didn't mean it, but tonight, I'd let loose some specifics. Maybe Gabe could help. Maybe that was the reason we'd met when we had. He'd had some traumas of his own. At least he could help me keep things in perspective.

Maybe my mom actually had talked about this stuff sometime in the past.

My back relaxed against my desk chair. For a moment, I wished I really were Deliverance so I could be in Salem and smack some sense into those people. After all, Martha Carrier was going to die and all because she had quarrels with neighbors who wanted her land. And then their cows would die, or they would get sick or get their hand stuck in farm equipment and blame it on her "specter." They just needed somebody to accuse because they didn't understand about germs, and because they believed accidents didn't happen to godly people without reason. For this, Martha was going to die.

I caught myself and felt goose bumps everywhere. Going to die? Martha was already dead for three centuries.

Get real, Delli. I warned myself nervously, spine wracking against my desk chair. Hoping none of the kids who sat near me had heard my little giggle. What I really wished I could do was help Deliverance save the swamp-man from the frantic mob. After all, she seemed to feel for him the sort of feelings I was starting to feel for Gabe. Not romance, not really. I simply liked him and wanted to protect him.

Then I reminded myself. It was all just dreams, after all.

9

Abby and Betsy hurried over to me after school so they could meet Gabe Wincott.

St. Bart's student body was small, and the interesting new senior was the hottest topic of the day. He was waiting for the "limo" with me on the grassy half-moon in the front of Swink Hall, the lovely brick administration building.

"Hi, Delli. I saw Gilles in Crafts Class, and he said to tell you hi," Abby announced cheerfully when she caught up to us. She totally looked at Gabe when she spoke, though, making sure he could hear her.

I doubted Gilles had said any such thing, but I knew Abby well. With the plan of pairing me up with Gilles van Nullens, Abby counted herself first in line to snag Gabe. She wanted him to think I was out of competition.

"Betsy, Abby, I'd like you to meet my new neighbor, Gabe Wincott."

The girls giggled a little after I introduced them, and Gabe took turns politely offering them a handshake. Abby touched his hand for a second longer than she needed to, but he didn't pull away or anything. It was actually a pretty suave thing to do. Most dudes we know would have tipped their head upward with a "wassup."

"Cool walking stick." Abby's eyes started to gleam, but Gabe was spared an answer. The Rolls pulled up then and he gallantly opened the door, waving me inside.

Looking over at the driver, he called out "Hey, Dad," his voice full of affection. I fought down my embarrassment at a senior boy getting picked up by his father with Abby and Betsy watching. A limo with chauffeur would have been quite the thing. But Gabe didn't seem mortified at all.

Abby's eyes started to shine brighter. She dashed over to the driver's side, wearing a huge smile.

"Hi, Mr. Wincott, welcome to our little corner of the world." Now Abby's eyes were big and blue like pansies, all wide and innocent, like they got when she tried to get a teacher to postpone a test or give her more time on an assignment. I groaned. I knew what was coming next because I could practically hear the wheels spinning inside her head. Abby was going to try to charm Mr. Wincott out of his new home.

Indeed, her pretty pink lips started to pout a little as the man greeted her. Mike Wincott was an interesting combination of Abby's dad and my own. Longish gray hair with several days of facial stubble like Chris, casual but *very* expensive clothes. Ferragamo loafers just like Abby's dad. But no socks, like mine.

"Now, Mr. Wincott, I'm Abby Goodman. I just found out that you bought the Lynch place." The pout puffed more. "Daddy has had his heart set on that land for years. He's gonna be so disappointed." Her eyelashes flitted like a dark blue butterfly.

Mr. Wincott smiled at her in a fatherly way. "Ah, so Tom Goodman's your dad. Yeah, we had some intense negotiations, but I wasn't about to give up. The location is perfect. I only have to get to my day job in

L.A. a couple days a week, so the commute isn't so bad, and I wanted Gabe out of the rat race."

Abby tried to laugh in understanding, but I saw the determined look in her eyes.

"Well, nice to meet you, Abby. Do greet your dad for me." Gabe's dad turned the key before she could say anything else. "You two buckled in back there?" He turned his head back a little to check on us. It made me feel kind of infantile, but I guess it was a sweet gesture.

As we drove off, I recognized Abby's dark look right off, but she waved anyway. For an awful moment, I suspected she wasn't done with either Wincott. And for that awful reason, I started to feel even more protective of Gabe.

For a while, father and son talked about the first day of school.

"You two have any classes together?"

"Nah, I'm a junior." I sort of wished Gabe did have American Lit with me. We could work on a project together, and I would have a better reason to get his input about my name on that newsletter. Without looking like a total nutcase.

Except, I remembered, the newsletter was messed up, and Mr. Gallindo didn't have the original. But maybe I could still find one of the photocopies somewhere. Betsy had said there were several.

"I'm way ahead in Calculus, but they're going to let me take a real-time televised course at the university. I really did have a great first day." Gabe smiled at me when he said it, and I felt a little bit wonderful deep in my tummy. The feeling sure beat yesterday's nausea. I sure didn't want to think about throwing up or anything else icky, especially not

Calculus.

"Cafeteria food is gross though." Gabe and his dad both guffawed with laughter.

Just hearing them, my stomach churned. That awful tomato juice. *God will give you blood to drink.* My throat started to gag, but I fought down the feeling, forcing my mind back to Gabe.

"I think I'm really going to like it there, Dad," Gabe was saying, and I mumbled something affirmative. "And our new neighborhood."

Again he looked at me and my heart moved a little funny inside my chest. But at least it wasn't beating a million miles an hour like those other times. And my stomach was just about normal.

You'll like it around here only if you don't get in Abby's way, I told him silently, almost disliking my best friend. But love is supposed to be unconditional. I decided to enjoy the moment and forget about icky things. The "limo" was already heading up Skyline Lane. Mr. Wincott would be dropping me off soon.

"Do you want to…come over for a while?" I asked Gabe shyly, not wanting us to be apart just yet.

"I was hoping you'd ask." His lids dropped halfway, and my heart fluttered like crazy.

As we reached my house, I started to seriously hope there were some doughnuts and normal soda pop left over from yesterday. If I had to serve Gabe some of Mattie's concoctions, he'd run screaming for home, and I'd never see him again.

"Well, it sounds like you like St. Bart's and the seniors. I'm really glad about that." I meant it.

"Yeah. The kids I met today are cool," he said as we walked up the driveway toward the kitchen entrance. His left hand knocked against my right a few times, and I hoped he'd grab my fingers and hold on. "But what's with you and Abby?"

When he asked that, I was glad we hadn't been holding hands, or I would have dropped his like a hot rock. "What do you mean?" I didn't like those little pretend bugs crawling across my skin again. *What did he mean?* Was he interested in asking Abby out, thinking he needed my permission first or something? I mean, it would have to be OK with me if that's what he wanted.

I just hope he didn't, that's all.

"What do you mean?" I asked again when he didn't say anything. Abby had seemed flirty with him earlier, but she'd looked pretty unhappy when they left school. Gabe hadn't been watching her though. He couldn't have seen her dark looks or known what lurked in Abby's mind about trying to get his dad to sell their place. Maybe he had some sort of sixth sense about her. "Do you like her?"

"Hmm." He held the screen door for me. No one else was around, but I rejoiced when I saw a perfectly normal bag of Cheetos on the kitchen table and some perfectly normal bananas. Not plantain ones. And there was sure to be cold water in the fridge if nothing else. It would be in one of Mattie's hand-thrown ceramic pitchers, though, not disposable individual bottles that pollute the environment. At least my mom doesn't use an old fashioned ice-box although she does mention them from time to time.

I was right. I poured two tall glasses and smiled as I handed one to him. We sat at the old Formica table.

"Let me ask you this. Why do *you* like her?" Gabe's voice was gentle but not his words.

Almost shocked at the question, my smile died like

a burst bubble, and I almost dropped my glass. His question was so absurd, so personal.

So none of his business.

"Well, she's my friend. My best friend." I didn't care if he watched my forehead crinkle in a frown. He was way out of line.

He shrugged a little now. "I just don't see it. Whenever I told people today you're my neighbor, they all seem to like you a lot. But they say Abby's like, sorta selfish and sneaky. They don't know why you hang around her."

"That's just gossip." On one level, I silently agreed with Gabe, thinking of Ms. Lipsett and Coach Clayter. However, it was important to remain loyal to Abby. That's what friends did. She'd had my back since the first day of freshman year. Then I remembered Abby's plans to mess with his dad to get him to sell. Maybe I ought to tell Gabe about that.

Well, I decided then and there that I might tell him someday, but today didn't feel like the right time. All Abby's little threat would do would make him hate her, and I really wanted them to be friends. I'd tell him only what he needed to know. Abby's mom wasn't a big secret. It wouldn't be disloyal to Abby to tell Gabe about Mrs. Goodman, and the ugly divorce was sure to help him understand Abby better.

"Well, Abby and I go back to our first day of ninth grade. None of my friends from middle school came to St. Bart's, so I didn't know anyone the first day. Unlike you." I tried to be a little flirty. "I was majorly scared."

"I get that." Gabe took a long sip of water but didn't seem compelled to say anything else.

I took an even longer sip. "Abby just...like, took care of me right way. Took care of Betsy, too," I said.

"Abs was so fun and friendly. We're all best friends forever now. And well, she won't mind you knowing." I took a look at him. He seemed interested. Because he had his own situations that could be misunderstood, I took a chance that he would give Abby the benefit of the doubt.

"Abby is having a terrible time right now. I think she acts all hard because she's hurting so much."

"Yeah?" he prompted.

"Last Christmas Eve, her mom stayed up until two in the morning, wrapping presents and stuffing stockings for the whole family. Like she did every year. Made a big old feast for about a jillion relatives the next day. Like she did every year. Mr. Goodman gave her a diamond bracelet which she put on and showed everybody. Like she really loved it and everything."

I looked away because I honestly did feel Abby's pain. Mrs. Goodman had always been so pretty and fun. The whole thing was so unimaginable. The Goodmans had been like a grownup Ken and Barbie. "Then on December twenty-sixth, Abby woke up, and her mom was gone. Took the diamond bracelet and a bunch of clothes and ran off with some guy she'd hired to refurbish the cedar paneling in all the closets."

I could still hear the screams over the phone when Abby called me. Horrible sounds. "No one's seen her since. She doesn't call Abby or anything." My voice was soft because I wasn't trying to talk over Abby's long ago howls.

"Wow. That's messed up." Gabe's eyes widened.

"Yeah. She's got some high-powered Beverly Hills divorce lawyer that all the stars use, but Mr. Goodman has a watertight pre-nup."

"That's crazy," Gabe said, shaking his head.

Right then I sort of wanted to know about his own mother, but I figured Abby was the more important subject in the conversation right now.

"I just feel extra bad for what she's going through. Maybe that's why I put up with some of her, well, crap. Since she was there for me when I needed somebody. But I know firsthand that she's got a good heart. And I mean that." I did, too, so fervently I reached for Gabe's hand and squeezed it.

Gabe made a sort of neutral sound in his throat. As he shrugged, my hand fell away and he made no move to reclaim it. Oh well, it wasn't a romantic moment at all, and he did seem like he was digesting what I'd told him.

And not disgusted that I'd touched him.

"Do you want something to eat?" I asked politely; glad to break the silence and move on to something else.

Gabe's long hair swirled around his shoulders as he shook his head. "Let's take a walk in the grove."

"Scat's really going to make you cut that hair off," I teased, wishing I'd dared touch his hair before it was gone. It looked sleek and smooth like black satin. Then I was glad he didn't want Cheetos. I really didn't like to eat in front of guys. Especially orange gunk that would get all over my fingers.

The wind had died down, and the day wasn't as hot as yesterday. Dad was right. The Santa Ana's seemed to last about three days at a time. In my book, the grove wasn't all that exciting, but it would be nice to do anything with Gabe right now. I could feel the warmth of his body as he walked close to me down the stone steps and the gravel path. He didn't even use his walking stick.

"You seem to be walking OK," I mentioned, hoping that I didn't sound nosy.

"Yeah. I think my doctors are really happy with my recovery."

"That's so great," I said, meaning it, but wishing I could think of something wonderful and sophisticated to say. After all, he'd met a lot of girls today who are a lot older and prettier than I am. Lots richer, too, although I don't think he cared about that.

"What's your dad's day job?" I remembered something Mr. Wincott had said in the car. How he had to go to L.A. a couple days a week.

"He owns a company that designs movie sets and scouts locations. He apprenticed on that Scottish movie I told you about. His first one. He plays the soundtrack all the time."

"Wow." I remembered the movie's theme song Gabe had played yesterday. The same notes that the disfigured man had played for Deliverance in the swamp. But my attention wandered. On the branches of one of the avocado trees, I saw it again, the yellow bird. My dad was going to be so happy that it had come back.

Maybe it was a good luck charm after all.

"Shhh, look. Over there," I told him quietly, walking carefully to get into a better position.

"What?"

"The prettiest yellow bird." I whispered to keep it close and unafraid. "I saw it yesterday. My dad thinks it might be a wild canary."

"Where?"

"There!" I pointed. "You can't miss it. It's like a flash of gold about fifteen feet away. Oh, no, there it goes. It's flying away!" I waved my hand, still pointing.

Gabe squinted then looked puzzled. "I don't see anything. Sorry."

That was impossible! The bird had been close enough for us almost to touch. Then I remembered. Gabe had mentioned that his vision still had some recovering to do. I better not make it a big deal.

"We've all been thinking my eyesight was almost back to normal." He sounded sad as he guided my elbow so we could walk farther. I held off the temptation to finally reach for his hand.

Hearing the remark, I shivered with confusion. That meant he ought to have seen the bird. Why hadn't he seen it?

Suddenly everything—the air, the breeze, the sunlight—seemed to hang on my skin too thick. My feet seemed to drag through the leaves and dust, the way Deliverance's feet had done in the swamp. A feeling of dread slowed the blood in my veins.

The yellow bird. *The devil's familiar.* Something the girls in the courtroom had seen, but nobody else.

Just then inside my head, I heard Reverend Parris's niece once again. She was yelling to the frantic crowd that she'd seen a demon in the swamp. Once again, I felt the desperate need to warn him.

Maybe tonight in my dream, Deliverance would reach the swamp.

Only…he and Deliverance lived in a three hundred year old dream. What I realized instead was that somehow, *Gabe* was in danger, too. He was the one I needed to warn.

I turned to him, troubled. He obviously thought I was worried about his eyesight, so all he said was, "Nah, don't worry, Delli. I'm getting better, really. I don't want you to...I don't want to scare you away."

"No, it's not that, Gabe. Not at all. It's just ... Abby's pretty mad at you folks for buying that old house. I don't know. I love her, but lately she gets into these moods."

He gave a bark of laughter. "I get it. You think she's going to pull some kind of prank. Well, I'll be fine, Delli. I promise. And my dad's a smart man. The Lynch house and all the dealings are just one of many."

As he spoke, he bent his head just like he was going to kiss me. But he stopped, grazing my cheek with his left hand instead.

I confess to being a little disappointed, but at last, he did take my hand and we walked under the shade of the trees for a while. His fingers were soft and warm.

Once I thought I saw the yellow bird again, flitting among some branches, but I didn't want to make him feel bad. I didn't say anything.

Unlike the girls in the courtroom.

10

The yellow bird landed on the branch of the swamp maple almost like it was a beacon of light.

Or of darkness. Deliverance reminded herself that the entire village of Salem now considered the man in the swamp a demon, if not the Dark One himself.

What if they were right?

The bird flitted onward. Shrugging against her good sense, she followed it, the edges of her skirts catching the fronds of fiddlehead ferns along the path. For once, her feet made good speed. This time the mud and muck didn't suck at the soles of her shoes. But would she find him before it was too late?

Had the Court of Oyer and Terminer remained in session after Abigail's outburst? If so, Deliverance's lengthy absence might be noticed. An extended visit to the privy would let the world think that she suffered some kind of symptom herself. And *that* could endanger her mother.

But then again, Abigail Williams's uncle Reverend Parris was a man of extreme action. Maybe the townsmen had banded together in quick pursuit. Maybe they were not far behind. Deliverance looked quickly back over her shoulder but heard and saw nothing.

What drew her to this monstrous man? Why did she long for another of his marks upon her wrist? Was it simply that he was forbidden her, like Tituba's fortune-telling? Was he her doom?

Was he leading her into temptation?

She did not know. What she did know was that she could not stay away.

Maybe his music would once again lead her to his side. She might call out to him if she knew his name.

But she didn't.

The heat of the August afternoon hugged her skin the way a woolen cloak did after rainwater had dampened it. She was thirsty, so thirsty. Ever since Goody Putnam's call for cool water, she had longed to take a drink. Right in front of her was a little pool. If it were not all that dank, she might chance a sip. It might be fed by a bubbling spring. She was wary of water. Everyone said it was the source of bad vapors but today she did not care.

Her throat was so dry.

Kneeling, she caught a glimpse of her reflection. Although mirrors were a thing of vanity, of evil, she smiled. Her face, dusted like nutmeg with freckles, peered back up at her with eyes the color of lavender. Shamefully, she realized she was comely.

She wondered if the young man she sought would think so. Another shameful thought. A flash of warmth tightened her cheeks. She remembered the true purpose of this venture. To warn him. Avoiding the murky water, she set off again.

A word left her mouth without thought. A name.

His name.

"Gabriel? Gabriel? It is you I seek! Where are you?"

Stunned, she found him in front of her, so close she had to brake her feet into the muck. Her breath caught in her dry throat like unchewed meat.

"How is it you know my name, mistress?" His low voice held the burr she remembered and had longed to hear again. This late afternoon, he wore a long black cloak. In the dank breeze, it flapped around his knees like bat wings.

How is it that she knew his name?

"I have no answer," she managed when her breath returned. "I longed to call out to you before, but had no name to use. Suddenly..." She wanted to shiver at the oddness of it, but instead gloried in the beauty of his half-face. As before, his endless black hair covered the ravages.

She looked at him straight on. "Suddenly the name came to me as if it were a miracle."

Or a spell. She held back a shiver as she reminded herself of that possibility as well. *How is it that she knew his name?*

"They are after you, Gabriel." Her voice was urgent. More pressing matters were afoot. "The good folk of Salem. I have just come from the courtroom. You have been seen. A frantic mob is setting out to...accuse you." She could not say the words "capture" or "hang."

She could not ask if he were archangel or devil.

Good or evil.

"I know." His voice was surprisingly calm. "I have expected this. But I have a good hiding place. Come along."

Without thought—and without fear—she let him take her hand. His fingers felt soft and warm.

He moved some branches of bracken and led her to the mouth of a small cave. "Go inside."

It was hard to trust. He had asked her to do so once, and she could not do it. Not then. Perhaps in a while. But not yet. She did not know where the cave led. Yes, perhaps in a while, if they heard the voices and shrieks of the mob. Then, yes then, she would follow him inside. Follow him anywhere.

But not yet.

He seemed to understand her hesitancy and took her to a large rock instead. Removing his cloak, he draped it across the rock. The edges of the flowing garment spread over the leaves on the ground. They sat, her on the rock, him on the ground.

"So tell me how you know this?" she asked. Her knees shook; she was glad to sit down. How could he sense things, know the unknown if he were not a man of darkness?

His head shook, rippling his hair through the air, as if to disavow her doubts. "There is no mystery to it. It always happens. I cannot live among people for long without causing them fear. So the good folk are moved to deem me a wizard or a demon. After a time, I move on to some other place."

"Then you must leave. You must go now!"

"I cannot." His one good eye stayed fixed on her as he told her simply.

"Why not?"

"You are here."

A strange thrill rippled down her spine. Remembering that her reflection had deemed her comely, she felt both cold and hot. He must think her comely, too.

But now was not the time, nor was this the place. In truth, she would not be considered old enough to wed until well into her twenties, but her honored mother would never allow it, anyway. Not to this disfigured stranger not of their faith and ways.

"You must leave, Gabriel. Now. You said before that you knew where to find me. I will still remain. You can find me somehow. Later. When Salem is safe again." Danger pounded through her veins. "You must leave here!"

"I will be fine, Deliverance. But Salem may not be safe for *you.*"

She knew that. Salem was not safe for anyone. She and her honored mother were constantly wary, always on guard. Right now, Deliverance wondered how he knew *her* name. It was just as mysterious as her knowing his. Too much of the unexplained prickled the back of her neck. She needed to leave now. Her skin itched with gooseflesh.

But she also wanted to remain with him, to learn about him. To know of this terrible thing that kept him hiding in deep forests and dank marshes, running from place to place.

"Why are you here? Who are you?" she asked him in a rushed, hushed whisper.

"I know you are daughter to Goodman Christian Wyllys, dead this past year, and his goodwife Matilda." He touched the edge of her cap. "I know that had we lived in better times, you would be mine."

Deliverance all but stamped her foot. "This is not about me. It is about you. So you know this of me. I know *nothing* of you."

He sighed. A waft of breeze caught the curtain of his hair, and for a brief instant, she saw again the carnage that had once been a face. She reached out, and he moved the hair purposely, and she touched the flesh. Closing her eyes, she found it warm and soft. It was only when she saw the destruction that she recoiled in horror.

He laid his hand on top of hers, keeping it atop his ruined cheek. "All right. I must hurry and be brief in case this mob is soon upon us. Well, I have been at the mercy of a mob once before. It is for you that I am afraid."

"Do not fear for me," she scolded, impatient. "The townspeople are my neighbors. The circle girls are my friends. Tell me your confidences. Please, Gabriel?"

Even though he had just mentioned hurrying, he looked away from her for a long time, like he fought for the words to speak.

"I was born a crofter's son, in the Highlands past Duntroon. A strong lad, stalwart beyond my years, faithful in the kirk of my fathers, and comely too, truth to tell. My laird's niece fancied me, but I knew my station, and I resisted her.

"Whoever had been her lover disavowed her when she grew heavy with child. Before she died in labor, she named me the father. Her cousins came after me, accusing me of casting a love spell upon her, for she ne'er would have coupled with a humble crofter's son."

His sigh lay in the thick air like a wisp of fog.

"My good and generous laird had been away at the Court of His Majesty Charles during these events. The mob decided to burn me for witchcraft. As the good grace of God would have it, my laird returned just in time to prevent the injustice. I had already been trussed to the stake. But before I could be untied, a flaming torch caught my face." He pulled our hands from his cheek.

"Not by mistake, I fear." The beautiful half-lips smiled grimly, "and the visage you see now was the unhappy result."

Wordless, Deliverance grasped his hand in fervor again. *He had mentioned God and His good grace. The kirk of his fathers.* Demons and devils did not speak of such things. They could not. Their lips could not form heavenly words. Surely, she could protect Gabriel from this new angry mob.

His voice had grown almost pensive. She knew why before he spoke. In spite of the evil charged against him, someone had believed in him then, had stood by his side. Just like she would stand by him now.

"Despite his own grief at his niece's loss, his horror at her lies trumped. My laird engaged a trusted physician to assist my wounds. After I had healed enough to travel, his generosity sent me to the New World, for he feared I would never be safe in the Highlands, marked as I am."

Now he laughed bitterly. "Unbeknownst he assisted me right into a hotbed of witchery."

Deliverance had no time to spend in commiseration. "Oh, this is a tragic story and an impossible coil. We must do something and lose no time. Gabriel, my mother is an honorable person of intellect. She will help us. I know it," she said with fervor before realizing she had used *us* thoughtlessly. "I meant, of course, she will help *you*. But…"

Angry sounds from the dark shadows behind them began to drum in her ears. She tightened her lids in prayer. "Oh, dear and generous Lord, in your Providence, delay the mob. Permit Gabriel's escape." Eyes wide, she pushed at Gabriel. "You must escape. You must go now. Perhaps I can think of an excuse and hold them off."

"Yea. I knew you would be my deliverance. My

Deliverance. I will come back for you. Wait for me. But first, with your permission. Although I must make haste but we have time for this."

He rose, pulling her up with him. For the first time, she realized the remarkable length and breadth of him. A strong, stalwart lad who had once been comely.

Her strong stalwart lad who was no demon, who rejoiced in God. Who would always be comely to her. She knew what he intended. For a moment, she remembered the mark his kiss had left on her wrist. If his kiss marked her like that again, she would face the gallows. She remembered that she should feel wanton and immodest.

But she threw all such notions into the dusk. He bent his face down to her, and his long hair covered her like a black veil.

Her neck almost hurt at the upward tilt of her chin.

A thunderous sound rang in her ears, and her stomach ached...

11

The phone was ringing off the hook, right into my ear. MTV was blaring. My neck had a crick in it for lying against the sofa arm. In my stomach, a load of canned spaghetti lay like a lump of Mattie's moist clay.

I'd had to pass on Mattie's parsnip stew, begging to eat with my nieces instead. But I hadn't been ready to eat anything red just yet. So I had rinsed off the tomato sauce when Mattie wasn't looking and eaten just the round noodles.

God will give you blood to drink.

I shivered.

Even with the wad of soggy pasta deep in my gut, I felt a little bit of relief. Another dream. That's all. Just when I thought it was safe to go into the water, or whatever that dumb expression was.

But this one made sense, at least. I had wanted Gabe to kiss me and he'd stopped, and the same thing had happened to Deliverance.

The phone rang again, and I grabbed it. I didn't even know what time it was.

"Can't somebody get that?" My dad yelled; something he rarely did.

"Got it, Dad." I yelled back.

"Delli? Aren't you in bed yet? It's almost ten." Mattie's voice chided from somewhere far off in the cavernous house. "Remember, you've been a bit sickly."

I ignored her. The phone was old fashioned and wired to the wall with a long curly cord. Gabe had called this number last night. My heart pounded. "Hello?"

"It's me." Abby chirped, not sounding tired at all.

"Hey." Hopes dashed.

"Why aren't you answering? I've called about a million times," she complained.

"I'm downstairs." I shrugged even though she couldn't see.

"Well, I just have to tell you the craziest thing."

I groaned. That wouldn't be anything unusual, coming from Abby, but I wasn't in the mood for much of her right now.

"Well, Daddy thinks I'm not responsible enough around here."

I didn't wonder. Since Abby's mom left and her sister went off to college, her dad had hired a whole militia of servants to take care of everything imaginable.

"So I'm gonna dog sit my neighbor's little rat dog while she goes on a cruise. I even get paid. Thing is, wanna help?"

I laughed out loud, the funny feelings and weird dream vanishing, at least for now. "I thought this was supposed to make *you* responsible. No, thanks."

I could practically hear Abby pouting over the wires.

"Come on, Abby. Get real," I ordered. "I mean, you never help me babysit McKenna and Gracey. Or when Mattie needed some extra help stocking shelves for her craft show last summer? Betsy helped. You stayed home."

"Sorry." Abby sniffed. "But your mom's little shop

can be weird. No offense."

"None taken." I sniffed back. Not true, though. Our whole family had gone pretty ballistic a few years ago when an anonymous letter in the weekly newspaper had criticized Mattie for stocking Aztec calendars.

But unease flashed through me at Abby's comment. It might not have, two days ago, before this Salem stuff. But it flashed bright and slimy right now. I didn't say anything else for a long minute.

Abby pouted through the phone line. I can't explain exactly what I heard, but it was the pout I heard often when we're face to face. "Oh, all right. I guess I can handle it. Pixie's about the size of a soda pop can."

"Yeah, I think you can do that," I said, waiting for Abby's real reason for calling. It had to be something about Gabe, his dad, or Gilles Van Nullens.

But it wasn't.

"I also decided to use my salary and get colored contact lenses."

"You don't even wear glasses." I couldn't believe her.

"Well, I've always wanted lavender eyes."

Lavender eyes? What on earth?

Well, my own eyes are green as grass. Then I remembered something from the dream. The loudmouthed circle girl causing so much trouble. Reverend Parris' niece. And Abby's own promise to yank Mr. Wincott's chain.

Wasn't the niece named Abigail?

"Hey, Abby, is your full name Abigail?"

She chirped happily again. "Nay and flay." Her version of no. "My christened name is Annabel. I guess

I couldn't say it when I was little. It came out 'abble' or something and just kind of turned into Abby. Why? Are you really Delli?"

She'd journeyed into undiscovered territory where I wasn't about to tread, so I cut the conversation short. No need to tie up the phone lines. Gabe might call to ask me to school again tomorrow.

But in the meantime, I had to know.

"Hey Abs, you're not still going to mess with Gabe and his dad, are you?"

"No, Delli. I'm over that. What do you think I am, like seven years old?"

"Well, yeah."

"Besides, Daddy already told me he's got his eyes on another place. He said Mr. Wincott was 'absolutely adamant' that he's not going to sell. Whatever 'absolutely adamant' means."

"It means he won't do it for any reason."

"Whatever." Abby hung up.

I held the receiver for a while longer, waiting for Gabe to call.

But he didn't.

~AΩ~

Alone with myself now, I relived the dream.

The reflection in the pond in the swamp had looked just like me. Well, what I saw in my mirrors, that is. And I guess what other people must see when they looked at me. Were the dream Deliverance and I the same person after all?

Except for those eyes. Lavender eyes—like Abby was going to buy. Imagine, wasting your dog sitting salary on some kind of lens that your eyes didn't even need. I for example would have saved the cash for Christmas presents.

Well, I wasn't the daughter of a rich man.

Then I remembered that man. That other Gabriel and his terrible face. I felt really bad about the misery the Highlanders had caused him.

Except he wasn't real and none of it had happened. My imagination had accelerated to an almost unbearable level. My parents had always encouraged me to write my ideas on paper, so I decided to do exactly that.

I'd write down these dumb dreams and make some sort of American Lit project out of them. In fact, I decided to start right then while the scene was fresh in my mind.

My feet felt heavy as I went upstairs, like Deliverance's sometimes did when she trudged through the swamp. I'd have to write about all that, too. Deliverance's feelings were always so real.

I propped myself on my bed and got a tablet and pencil from my nightstand drawer. I do have a desk in my room, but I always do schoolwork on my bed, even rough drafts before I word process them. Mattie always claims a rigid desk restricts creative flow, and I guess I've grown to believe it. I know she would have home schooled me if Dad hadn't put his foot down. Nothing against it, but he wanted me exposed to other authority figures.

I laughed out loud. So I get Scat.

"Lights out." Mattie appeared at the door, bearing tea and a warm scone of a different color. "After some nourishment, that is. This will all help you sleep." She set a steaming cup down on the nightstand.

"Aw, Mattie."

"Your health hasn't been the best these past two days, and I don't want to worry about you. I put some valerian in the tea, and the scone. My, my, try it."

"It's pink," I said cautiously. My tummy churned a little. What if the color had something to do with tomato juice? *God will give you...* "What's in it? Cherry cola?"

Yeah right.

"My own recipe. Some whole grain rye flour with a touch of pureed cranberry. Plenty of iron."

"Mom—Mattie—thanks, but could you leave me alone? I've got homework to do, and I'm not hungry."

"Well, you should be." Mattie huffed as she bustled toward the door. She's not a large woman, but she always wears long full-ish skirts and that's just how she moves. At the doorway, she turned to me and shuddered. "All that's in your belly now are those rancid round pastas. I just want you to get a good night's sleep. I love you, honey."

"Thanks, Mom. I love you, too." I meant it; she had a good soul. For a while, though, I ignored her suggestions and scribbled as fast as I could. Finally, I caved. The scone actually smelled good, something of a first, so I ate it. But I did leave the tea.

And I couldn't get to sleep even after my eyes and fingers got tired and I'd climbed into bed. For almost two hours, I had tried to construct all of Deliverance's actions and feelings for my project. But tired or not, for the rest of the night, all I did was doze lightly for a few minutes off and on. My room was hot and stuffy. Maybe that's why.

At least I didn't sleep long enough or deep enough to dream anything new. I had to believe Deliverance and her swamp man had gotten away from the angry

Anya Novikov

mob.

If they hadn't, well, I didn't want to know.

Just before dawn, when night started to turn gray, I'd had enough of my hot stuffy room. I'd never felt like doing this ever before, but I wanted to go down the hill to the avocado grove. I *needed* to go down the hill to the avocado grove.

Where I'd first met Gabe.

The fresh air would do me good even if it was a weird thing to be doing. I admit that right off. And while I was furious that he hadn't called or invited me to drive to school with him again, I was glad he's my friend and wanted to recall the good feelings.

After I dressed in shorts and a tank top, I headed through the quiet house and out into the remaining shadows. Not a breath of wind anywhere.

It was still more night than day, so I walked carefully down the stone steps and the gravel path. For a second, I remembered Deliverance's walk through the dark gloomy marsh. How brave she had been. How majorly brave not to run when she saw the stranger.

How quickly the stranger had appeared in front of her. Like magic. Or a spell.

I shivered but reminded myself of the morning chill. The Santa Ana Winds might bake Southern California in the fall, but the dawns could be dewy and cold. And ahead of me, I saw it.

Him. My heart jumped into my throat and stayed there.

A figure stood in the shadows of two trees, a black cape wrapped around him like bat wings.

12

"Delli? Delli! I knew you'd be here. I knew you'd come."

My heart still wasn't beating right, but it moved from my throat down to the cavity where it belonged. I did find that I was able to talk.

"Gabe? What on earth are you doing here? What's wrong? What's going on?" My feet felt rooted into the leaf-covered ground.

"I can't explain it. I just..." He looked down at me, the look on his face almost like a naughty puppy who'd peed in the house. What was going on?

"I couldn't sleep," he said.

"Neither could I." I confessed. "I needed some fresh air. But what are *you* doing *here*?"

"I needed to talk to you. To see if you're all right. I was worried."

"Why?" Being worried about was kind of fun, but this whole scene was so bizarre I felt mostly on edge.

"I couldn't call and wake up everybody. I just...knew you'd come." He slipped the cape off his shoulders and spread it across the stump and ground, like the swamp man had done for Deliverance.

I shivered, but this time it wasn't just the dawn and dew.

"I don't understand, Gabe. What on earth is that vampire cape for?" I wanted to make a joke of it but I really couldn't. This was all too, too bizarre. "It won't be Halloween for a month. And we're not eight years old anyway."

"I don't know. I don't." In the gray, I saw his eyebrows rise. "I passed a costume shop yesterday and wanted it. When I left the house a few minutes ago, I figured the morning would be chilly. It was hanging there on the hall tree. By the door."

Weird. Way weird. I did want to turn and run back to the house, but mostly I wanted to stay. This was Gabe, after all.

Besides, Deliverance had stayed to hear what the swamp man had to say.

"I get these feelings sometimes." Gabe motioned me to the stump, and he sat on the ground. "Feelings of doom, I guess. But the thing is, they mean something."

"What?"

"When I get one of those feelings, I've learned not to ignore it. I had one, for a couple days before I collapsed. I never told my dad about it. It wasn't just the dizzy spells. I mean, I felt terror. Pure terror. It happened once before that. When my mom died."

"Oh, Gabe, I'm so sorry."

"Well, you don't really need to be. That's what makes it so whacked out. I didn't even know her. She and my dad never got married. She didn't want me, so he paid her to, well, give birth. He wanted a kid." Gabe sounded kind of embarrassed. "Then she disappeared. But when I was thirteen, I guess she figured I would do a bar mitzvah or something, and she called and wanted to see me.

"Well, she was Jewish, but Dad and I are Christians, so I wasn't having a bar mitzvah. But Dad was OK with her coming over, and at first I was all excited." He tried to chuckle, but I could hear his voice thud. "Then this feeling came. And she died in a plane crash coming to see us.

"So now I don't take the feeling lightly. Something's going to happen, Delli. Something bad. Something *now*."

"Oh, Gabe, no. It isn't." I tried to comfort him, but how could I? I'd been feeling pain and terror three hundred years old myself. Then I realized I couldn't do it on my own. "Let's turn to God. Let's pray." I folded my hands together.

His long hair drifted over his shoulders, and he looked down at me. "I just couldn't take a 'no' from Him. Not about this."

"Prayer does work, though," I said, tightening my fingers in firm belief. "I mean, the answer may be no, or not now, but God doesn't ignore us."

"Well, I hope His answer to this isn't a no or a not now." Pain flashed across his face.

"What do you mean? Are you having symptoms? A setback? You told me you're getting better. You said so." I snapped my fingers although whenever I tried, they never made a sound. The motion kept me from taking his hand. "Do you mean you're getting sick again? Or that something will happen to your dad?"

"No, Delli. Something's going to happen to *you*."

The swamp man had told Deliverance he was afraid for her. I wanted to be angry, but part of me warned myself not to be.

"What are you saying, Gabe?" My voice squeaked with panic. I'd have to pray later about alleviating it, about trusting God, but right now, Gabe's words terrified me. "What on earth do you mean?"

"I don't know what it is or when. But it'll be

soon." His voice was calm. "I'll pray. I'll pray for your safety. But you be on guard, too."

The devil is no more real than when he's an angel of light.

Then something I'd remembered myself as a threat smacked every brain cell I have inside my skull.

Deliverance Wyllys. Hanged September 24, 1692.

My stomach heaved again, regretting the scone. *Two days from now.* Well, two days from now three hundred years ago. But I managed to hold the bile down. Ann Putnam had barfed in front of a whole town, but I wasn't about to do it, even in front of just one guy.

Even if he deserved it. Besides, of course I didn't mean two days from now. I meant, three hundred years ago. The dates were nothing but coincidence.

I was angry at him now rather than scared. How could a Christian *not* trust in God? Even when I didn't, I knew I was supposed to and would get back on track. For some reason, Gabe wanted attention. He wanted me to think I needed him. And then I was angry at myself. For a time, I had needed him. Needed his take on what was going on. Now, he'd ruined everything.

All I truly needed was God.

"This is…is just totally crazy. I'm going to go back home and try to rest a little then get ready for school. You're not very nice, Gabe. I didn't deserve this. I thought you were my friend. I even told you about Abby and her possible pranks."

"That's why I'm here with you now. Delli, wait."

But I didn't.

~AΩ~

Even though I had time for a couple more hours of rest and probably could have used it, I didn't want to go back to bed. Why in the world would I want to go to sleep and dream more of those awful dreams? But I was so, so tired. Besides, if Mattie found me wandering around restlessly, who knows what weird herbal dosages she would inflict on me?

But then it dawned on me. Maybe I ought to trust Mattie more, talk to her. God had placed me in a wonderful family that didn't run from feelings or ideas or make you feel dumb if you stood out in the crowd. And Deliverance herself seemed to place high value upon her mom. What did she call her? Honored mother? That was pretty high praise, and I felt a little bit self-conscious. Normally I thought Mattie was a half-teaspoon short of full. But maybe I ought to trust my mother. Yesterday I had thought that Gabe might be the one to confide in because of his unusual circumstances.

Wrong.

And Mattie had surrounded herself with the unusual her entire life.

Oh well. Maybe things would look a little brighter in the morning. All I planned to do was close my eyes, just for a few minutes. For some reason, I found a floppy chewed-up stuffed toy dog on the floor by my bed. McKenna or Gracey must have dropped it. I picked up the ratty thing. It was surprisingly nice and soft, so I hugged it like I was four-years-old again and climbed into bed.

~AΩ~

"There was a dog." Reverend Parris's frail little

blonde daughter shrieked. Deliverance watched in terrible fascination as the child moaned and twitched. Once healthy and friendly, she had been the first of the girls afflicted. "A witch of a dog. The devil's disciple. It passed me in the street yestermorn and gave me the evil eye."

"I know such a cur," someone called out. "A miserable stray that Goody Good used to befriend. Her *familiar*. Sarah Good used her familiar to confer with Satan himself. We must hang that dog."

The plan was greeted with a hundred gleeful shouts.

After he settled the tumult, Judge Hathorne tapped his nose thoughtfully. "In truth, Goodwife Good brought the smallpox to our town," he said. "She let her own babe die whilst she served her prison time. Such a mongrel could certainly be her assistant. Her familiar."

"In truth, she deserved hanging for her witchery," another declared righteously. "So does that dog."

"But did Bridget Bishop deserve such a death, she who nursed our township during the smallpox? Did *she*?"

This was a female voice that Deliverance couldn't identify at first. Instead, she wondered who would be so foolhardy to speak such dissent. In horror, she realized it was her own honored mother.

But Matilda Wyllys spoke for only her daughter to hear.

"Be cautious." Deliverance warned, squeezing her mother's hand. "I beg you. Who knows what ears even these walls have?"

Then, the circle girls shrieked anew. The courtroom exploded in a fury of new accusations and names as the girls remembered neighbors' bad habits and vices, old grievances that had never been settled. Even as Deliverance shivered with terror for herself, for all those innocent, her heart hurt for a poor, hungry dog whose only fault was taking food from a witch. She and Patience had petted it once, but their mother had refused to allow the cur inside their house, fearing fleas.

She remembered its soft tongue lick her with affection. With gratitude.

"Hang the dog! Hang the witch's familiar!" screamed the little Parris girl as she flailed wildly some more. Her cousin Abigail howled like a wolf.

"Reverend Parris, please," thundered Judge Hathorne, quieting the crowd. "You and your good wife, please attend your little Betty and your sister's child."

~AΩ~

Judge Hawthorne's loud order woke me. I shivered just like Deliverance in the dream. McKenna was pulling at the ratty soft stuffed dog, but I didn't really pay any attention.

Betty. It was awfully like Betsy. And Abby. Were these names just coincidence, too?

And now my two friends were in charge of taking care of a poor helpless dog.

13

By the time I had showered the strange night from my body, I felt better. I had reached an important conclusion. I couldn't really talk to Mattie.

My mom was certain to think my dreams were fodder for a series of intellectual lectures at the bookshop. And I already knew she'd advise me to humble myself before the Lord and beg Him to walk with me.

My dad wouldn't do, either. He had too much on his mind with the grove. And Angie...she didn't say a single word on the drive to St. Bart's and didn't even offer to stop at the Cruller.

I knew why. The morning news had a report about an Iraqi plane allegedly crossing into the no-fly zone toward a formation of Air Force F-15 Eagles. Glen was an airman, so Angie had a lot more important stuff on her mind than weird old Gabe.

And my stupid dreams about girls who lived three centuries ago were not real.

Instead, I tried to figure out what I would say to Gabe when I saw him again. Even though I was still mad, I did want us to be friends. And while I thought, for some reason, I kept hearing the swamp man's warning to Deliverance: *You must beware the circle girls. They are not your friends.*

Pooh. Poo-poo, doo-doo. Pooh some more. I sniffed in disgust. Deliverance hadn't been hanged. If she had even been real. She and Gabriel had obviously gotten away. The Puritans' careful records made no mention of her execution. Relief moved through my veins whether the two of them had been real or not.

Then I felt really super lame. I had started to worry and care about these—these figments of my imagination as if they were real people or something. Or worse, some mental soap opera characters who made me long for the next installment—which was as dumb as crying at the movies where everybody was fictitious, too.

I didn't think I was going nuts. And I did have God. God who promised never to forsake me. Now that was real.

I realized I ought to find Gabe. He was someone alive and real even if I was mad at him. In some way, I had started to care about him.

But he wasn't at school. Now care and anger turned to fear. He had been expecting something bad to happen. Maybe something had. He'd warned me, but after all, his feelings hadn't ever come true before. If so, his mom would have taken another flight. His doctors might have been able to prevent his illness.

Maybe that was it. Maybe his feeling of doom had brought about a relapse. Not a bad one of course, but something that needed to a quick checkup at the doctor.

By the time I stumbled into Mr. Gallindo's class, I was ready to fall asleep on my feet in spite of my worry for Gabe. The restless night was paying me back, and playing my rear off in P.E. hadn't helped a bit. I'd worn myself out making two goals.

Josh Taggart had kind of bunched his letterman's jacket into a big glob atop his seat back. Maybe if I arranged myself just right, I could hide behind it and catch some Z's. For whatever strange phenomenon, I seemed to have a heads-up in the Salem lectures anyway.

Amazing how my forearm was as soft as a pillow, thanks to Mattie's latest aloe and comfrey goo. I got my head positioned just right, scrunched behind Josh.

But as soon as I closed my eyes, I heard Betty Parris's voice again. *It was a witch of a dog. The devil's disciple.* Once again, I realized I should have taken the lost, starving dog home. It's only fault was taking handouts from a witch. I remembered that its matted fur had been surprisingly soft. I recalled how my mother's pennyroyal remedies could have soothed the torment of the fleas.

"Delli?" Mr. Gallindo was calling on me. I woke with a start. Oh. Mr. Gallindo was good. I'd forgotten that he had all-seeing eyeballs. His voice was amused and annoyed at the same time.

What had I been thinking? Well, dreaming? It had been *Deliverance* with the poor dog, not me! To save myself, I mouthed the first thing that came into my head.

Well, it was still *in* my head!

"The devil's familiar," I shot in the dark. There had to be some reason I'd had a two-second dream about the poor dog. "Like yellow birds and even dogs. Since the Puritans believed you couldn't talk directly to Satan, the so-called witches communicated through an animal called the devil's familiar."

"Right on, Delli." Mr. Gallindo glowed. "Two dogs were even hanged."

My little nap was forgotten. Two? I felt sick, wishing I'd taken the stray home. Well, of course, once again I meant *Deliverance.* Who at least had felt compassion for the poor creature, too.

I really wished I'd kept my mouth shut and tried to be a sit-down comic with a one-liner about sleeping in class. If Mr. G. got any more impressed with me, he was going to ask Chris or Mattie to be a guest lecturer. After all, there had to be some reason that I was having all this foreknowledge.

As it was, the class was looking at me with a lot of interest. Even though I get really good grades and all, I normally don't participate much in class. Josh led the herd in a round of applause, then he turned to me while Mr. Gallindo got the class under control.

"Hey, Del. Let me in on your secret. How I can sleep in class and still give Mr. G. the right answers?"

I laughed, too, and shrugged. If he knew my secret, he'd either think I was nuts or on drugs. So would anyone. But another bad feeling grew, and I couldn't stop it.

Tensing against the hard back of the desk chair, I raised my hand for once, unlike Josh Taggart who yammered out loud at will. I ought to verify the names in the dreams. "Mr. Galindo, what did you say the name of the reverend's daughter was?"

"Betty. Little Elizabeth Parris. And her cousin was Abigail or Abby Williams. But young Ann Putnam was believed to be the true ringleader, paying back the enemies of her mother, Ann Senior."

Hmm. I digested that for a second. Betty—or Elizabeth. Abigail. Ann.

You must beware the circle girls. They are not your friends.

Nah. Gabe was crazy. These girls were my friends. Besides, Abby, my Abby, was really Annabel. Kind of a mix of Abigail and Annabel.

Nah.

And Betsy…well, I tsked. Betsy wasn't Elizabeth at all but Betony.

No way. Still the dream about the poor dog bugged me. I almost whispered to Josh how soft the dog's fur had been and how my mother's pennyroyal could have soothed the poor creature's fleas.

My mother. I'd never petted the dog that had met an unholy end over three centuries ago. Of course, I meant *Deliverance* and the honored *Matilda.* Even still, an awful dread spread a sudden heat through my body. That little dog Pixie was now under Abby's care. I knew Betsy wouldn't be far behind. The two of them were certain to create some sort of havoc.

Fortunately, Josh Taggart brought me back to the matters at hand.

"What happened to those girls?" he asked. Fortunately, his jacket smelled more like a locker room than something named pennyroyal, so I knew I was back home again. "Did anyone ever know they were faking?"

Mr. Gallindo balanced himself on the edge of his desk before replying. "Answer to question one: Nothing. But about fourteen years after the hangings, Ann Putnam Junior did confess and offer an apology of sorts.

"And in answer to Question Two: it may be that not all their visions, their retching, the choking, the pricking sensations were fake."

"Whah?" Josh at his most eloquent.

Mr. Gallindo's voice lowered dramatically. "These symptoms just might have been real." He got up from his balancing act to write a long word on the white board.

"Ergotism." He pronounced it as he turned to face the class. "Caused by a chemical that can induce hallucinations and physical symptoms like LSD."

"Those girls were whacked out on drugs?" This time, Josh sort of raised his hand first.

"Maybe, but they didn't know it." Mr. Gallindo nodded. "It's a possible theory. Wet weather may have caused 'convulsive ergotism,' a disorder resulting from the ingestion of contaminated rye grain. Ergot is spread by a fungus that causes just these symptoms, and for some reason, females and young children were more likely to be poisoned than males."

"Huh?" I think we all gasped as one.

"There were even reports that some of the bread baked had taken on a pinkish hue," Mr. Gallindo said. "Just the right color for blood sacraments at witches sabbaths..."

My heart beat too fast, but that was pretty much the norm lately. And my warm skin heated up big-time. Again, not unusual these past days. I had odd visions, well, dreams. I remembered Mattie's pink scones. My mom railed against preservatives and pesticides and imported our family staples from the back of beyond.

No. I settled myself down. Gabe was the real and only cause of concern right now.

Mattie had used pureed cranberries, after all. She'd told me so.

~AΩ~

During break, I found out what a snake pit of gossip St. Bart's could be, maybe always had been.

Despite its name, the school is non-sectarian. It hadn't bothered me before because my family has a tight grasp of God, but maybe if it had been religious, if we'd had nuns or Bible classes or devotions, the mean girls might have climbed aboard the nice train and the cool dudes might have deserved their adjective. Suddenly I felt ashamed to be here, a place of status and high achievement.

"Where's your new boyfriend?" Abby asked, her wide eyes full of fake innocence as she directed us to the soda machine during the nutrition break. Obviously healthier habits were a thing of the past, but just thinking of the tomato juice turned my stomach.

God will give you…

Of course, Abby already knew that I hadn't come to school with Gabe.

"He isn't my boyfriend."

"Well, bet you wish he'd ask you to homecoming. Even though Gilles is more your style. Dang, Del. That lame walking stick. Gilles is *so* continental."

"Don't call me Del. I'm not even thinking about homecoming," I said, hot, "And I don't have or need a boyfriend."

"Liar!" Abby's smirk deserved to be sandpapered off her face.

I ground my teeth in my best imitation of her. "Why don't you go with Gilles yourself if he's so hot?" Turning my back to her, I dug in my backpack for some loose change. A Sprite might settle my stomach, and it wasn't remotely red.

"I have my eyes on a bigger prize." Abby's eyes narrowed, naming the student body president. I giggled to myself. Just what would happen if the big man on campus told her no?

Or worse, if I said the same to Gilles? A chill rushed across the nerves in my face. Abby did not like to be thwarted.

Betsy had tossed a bunch of quarters in the slot, her feet tapping impatiently "Everybody's saying your new boyfriend is in court today." She whimpered in a sappy way I'd never heard before. "Apparently he's wiggling out of a DUI."

My worries shifted. I could hardly believe my ears. "What on earth are you talking about?"

"It's all over school. Why else would a great big boy have his *daddy* drive him to school in the morning? 'Cuz he got his license to drive taken away! That's why."

"And that walking stick..." Abby popped the top of her soda. "He's probably still shaky from rehab."

My hands shook in rhythm with my head. I did the best I could. I wanted to set them straight, but I remembered my promise. I couldn't, not without Gabe's permission.

"You are both so lame. Just shut your pie holes. His dad is bringing him until he gets his California driver's license. They just moved here from out-of-state. And, FYI, he's got a dental appointment this morning. Now, you"—I pointed an index finger at Abby so my lies seemed more authoritative. "You just stop making up stuff. You told me you were over messing with Gabe and his dad."

Abby smirked. "I didn't make up the rumor. I just spread it around."

Right then the warning bell rang for the third period class, and we all headed toward Small Hall. Yes, I'd made stuff up, too, but only for a good cause. I couldn't let Gabe down, and I reckoned God would understand.

"Yo Bets. Compadre. You're helping me with Pixie after school, right? The great PETA supporter here"— Abby waved a few careless fingers at me—"has declined to participate in my great adventure." She gave us air kisses before she pranced off.

I shook my head at Abby's silly display. Louder than ever, the warnings of both Gabriels pounded in my ears.

14

By lunch time, the rumor mill was grinding full steam ahead. The cafeteria buzzed "details" about the new kid's addictions. Abby wasn't doing much to contradict the gossip, and I didn't have her clout.

"Why don't you help him?" I fumed to Abby. "You know all this is nonsense."

"I don't know any such thing. Besides, I might like being a member of his fan club—and yours, by the way—if you'd help me with Pixie and show some interest in Gilles."

I had had enough. "For your information, Gilles hardly ever acknowledges that I am alive. If he ever asks me a question, I'll have an answer. Besides, none of this is your business. And, *by the way*, Pixie *is* entirely your business!"

I didn't feel much like eating. But even the worst cafeteria food was better than whatever Mattie packed for me in a reusable linen drawstring sack she had woven. So I took my tray of seared salmon tacos over to Lesley Lebental, another girl that I could stand most of the time.

Still, I was as furious as I was astonished. How had a stick that had been "jaunty" only yesterday become an instrument of ridicule and suspicion? How could a dude who had been so cool twenty-four hours ago have descended into walking weirdness?

Just because his dad had driven him to school?

Well, I'd judged him wrongly, too. Shame flooded my face.

Lesley wasn't all that much of a talker, which was good, so I ate quietly by myself, thinking things through. I remembered the fat kid our freshman year. He'd been pretty cool about all the jokes and insults that came his way. Not until he died during Thanksgiving vacation did the fine, properly brought-up student body of St. Bartholomew's Prep School learn that he'd suffered from something called cardiomyopathy. The medicines that had tried to keep his heart alive hadn't been kind to the shape of his body.

Of course, the student body had properly mourned and gnashed their teeth, mostly because school let off a whole day for the funeral. But obviously they hadn't learned.

Parents paid a lot so their kids could have small classes. If they could all believe something so way uncool—before noon yet—maybe I could stop some of the nonsense by the end of the day. Lesley was quiet but pretty influential.

"Hey, Les, about Gabe. My neighbor," I began.

"You better steer clear," she interrupted. She leaned close; the stallion on her non-uniform designer polo shirt practically jumped in my face. She didn't bother to lower her voice. "AIDS."

I truly wanted to throw up the salmon tacos, all over her. "AIDS? Are you crazy? You don't know anything," I spat back, wishing everyone would leave me—and Gabe—alone. Wishing I knew where he was.

Almost wishing I'd never met him.

"Oh, and I suppose you do?" Abby set her tray down, all flouncy and prissy.

Of course I did, but I remembered my promise to Gabe. It would likely help him right now to share the truth about his condition, but he'd have told me it was OK to do that—if he'd wanted me to. After all, he knew all about rumors, even the AIDS one, and had survived them before.

I kept my mouth shut about him but tried to get the group to be reasonable.

"No," I lied. "I don't. But I do know that it's pretty bogus to believe rumors and make judgments about people. Remember Raymond?"

Total blank looks.

"...who had the heart attack freshman year?" I finished dramatically.

"Oh, the fat guy?" Shrugs.

"Yeah, the guy who *died*!" I yelled. I hadn't had much of an appetite to begin with, but watching Abby and Lesley smear food across their plates instead of really eating any of it made me gag. Not only because kids all over the world didn't have enough to eat, but because the day's menu turned an alarming color of red when mushed together. Salmon, raspberry compote, cherry pie.

God will give you blood to drink.

Swallowing hard, I didn't bother saying anything else. What was the use? I'd make a polite getaway soon. Maybe there *was* something to be said for home schooling.

"He still could have worked out or something." Abby stood up and did a couple of faux jumping jacks while Betsy and Lesley nodded vigorously. "It couldn't have hurt."

At that, I pushed the tray away and got up.

"You're all terrible people!" I accused, glaring

especially at Abby. "When you have a bad heart, you can't really exercise."

The circle girls are my friends.

Even as I watched Abby smile indulgently at me, like I was a cute little kitty who'd scratched the couch, my skin prickled uneasily. As I left the cafeteria, I heard them chanting their version of the old kiddie song, "Delli and Gabe, sitting in an avocado tree..." But then they used a profanity and Mr. Schnarch, who had lunch duty, yelled at them. Technically a word like that meant detention, but it was Abby, after all.

The poor motherless girl. My heart could still tug. I figured that the profanity had been her idea, but I knew Abby, and the rest, would be all normal and air-kissy by the time they saw me again, the incident cute and forgotten.

But for me, things would never be the same.

~AΩ~

It was a good day for gossip at St. Bart's. By the last period, everyone knew that Ms. Lipsett had been suspended.

For the time being, Mrs. Mergen, the counselor, was covering the Morality and Ethics classes.

"Can you believe it?" Josh Taggart whispered, pretty quietly for him. He and I also had U.S. History together. "She's a hooker! Scat just found out!"

"How?" Leered another jock sitting close by. "He's one of her tricks or something?"

"Oh, shut up, both of you," I demanded quietly, although I wanted to scream. "She's a cocktail waitress at a very nice restaurant."

"Same difference," yawned the jock. "Anybody

who dresses like a 'ho' might as well be one."

I fumed as my brain chugged thoughtfully. This desk felt hard and miserable against my backside. Maybe St. Bart's wasn't the place for me. I'd done more than a bit of adjusting my freshman year, settling in among a lot of rich kids with overly indulgent parents. Often I'd been unsure if I was proud or ashamed of my oddball parents, but Abby, bless her heart, had adored them. And that was that. For a second, I wondered why the student body hadn't pointed me out as strange and absurd? Was it simply because Abby had taken to me instead of inciting gossip?

You see, I knew full well that Abby was the source of this latest rumor. Classes had each been shortened a little to make time for a pep rally before school ended. I hunted Abby down before going over to the gym.

Abby was at her locker, moaning to Betsy about Pixie the dog.

"I don't know why I even agreed. I mean, I loathe rodents. Now, if Pixie was a *real* dog like a Labrador or a Golden something." Her voice trailed off miserably.

Betsy filled the tragic silence. "Now, c'mon. It'll be cool. I already told you Pixie can come over and play with our dogs."

I shook my head in disgust. "How much is she paying you, Bets?" I asked, pretty nastily, "or are you doing it because you love animals?"

Betsy blushed.

"And you, Lavender Eyes." I turned angrily on Abby. "You took on Pixie because Daddy asked. Same as Ms. Lipsett, right?" One more time I shot in the dark here, pretty sure my instinct was correct. Ms. Lipsett's suspension had more to do with Mr. Goodman than the D his daughter had gotten. Abby was just his little mouthpiece, his little puppet. He was using her to cast the stones of revenge.

Abby turned almost the same color as her desired eyes. Suddenly, I knew for sure what was going on. "I'm right, huh? Your daddy asked Ms. Lipsett out on a date, or worse, and she refused him. That's it, isn't it? Isn't it, Abby?"

Abby did her flounce thing, her lips tight as she said, "You don't know anything." But she didn't deny it and walked away, her rear going side to side like the pendulum of a clock.

Suddenly I looked across the wooded campus. With the same bright intensity of the first time I'd seen the dream man in the swamp—the rays of the sun pointing down on him like the treetops had a hole in them—I saw Gabe walking toward the gym. To get to him, I was like a salmon swimming upstream. Everyone else was going the opposite way.

"Gabe, where have you been?" I was so relieved I almost hugged him. Then I wondered how best to explain that he'd entered the St. Bart Snake Pit.

"Hi, Delli." He was shaky, leaning on the stick, but he seemed pale and interesting, not hopelessly addicted or dying of AIDS. Maybe Abby would keep her word, about Gabe at least, and quash the rumors.

"Are you all right?"

"Well, you of all people know what an awful night I had," he reminded me. "Thanks for being there for me."

"You're so welcome. I couldn't sleep either. It was nice to have someone I could go to." I didn't mean it, entirely. Just remembering that morning was still causing me some hackles of doubt and fear.

"Yeah. Sorry I couldn't bring you to school today.

Dad wanted me to see Dr. Stankowski about my anxiety."

Dr. Stan was a respected psychiatrist in town.

"Did he help?" I wanted to know but didn't want to be nosy.

"Well, I could take something for it," Gabe admitted, starting to stroll to the gym, "but my dad's not big on medication. He was, well, heavy into the drug culture early in his career and he's really careful about, you know, long term drug use. They're thinking about self-hypnosis. Who knows?" He shrugged, trying to make the whole thing seem light.

"Could you pray?"

He smiled down on me. "Sure. You don't get knocked to the mat by AVM and not have God help you."

"But you sounded so sad and doubtful in the grove."

"Because I'm worried about someone else."

My doubts thawed somewhat. "Then I'm sure you'll all decide on the best thing. And just so you know, my parents won't even use aspirin after the— shall I say—experiences of their youth." I couldn't help a choke and a chuckle. My folks used their own foibles, now regretted, to warn us against similar mistakes and misbehaviors. "My mom makes us willow bark tea. It's like liquid aspirin."

"Cool." He seemed like his jaunty self again. "Anyway, Dr. Stan is a good guy. But I missed you."

Like before, he bent close, almost like he was going to kiss me. But two things stopped him. First, Mr. Schnarch came out of his classroom with the command, "No public displays of affection on this campus. Now get to the pep rally."

"OK." Then Gabe asked him, "Can I get my homework first? I had a doctor's appointment this morning, and I missed your class."

"Sure." Mr. Schnarch and Gabe disappeared into the classroom.

Second, I realized that Abby had come back and stood like a statue a few feet away.

For an unhappy instant, I stood transfixed myself. How long had Abby been there? What had she seen and heard?

That Gabe had almost kissed me, that he had missed me—while Gilles Van Nullens was still in Abby's little mental video?

That Gabe's dad had been involved with drugs, my own had experiences too?

That he was seeing Dr. Stan, a well-known shrink?

Abby's eyes were bright, her voice false. "I came to tell you that I was sorry for being rude."

"Yeah." My voice and spirits were low. "Whatever."

Nothing about today was going well. But suddenly Abby's smile was true, real. She took my hand and squeezed it. "I mean it, Delli."

And I believed her even though Abby scuttled off quickly when Gabe appeared with his homework assignment.

~AΩ~

The pep rally was both a celebration of St. Bart's fall sports teams and a presentation of the senior girls nominated for homecoming queen.

I groaned. Now Abby, Betsy, Lesley and all the rest would consume their days and weeks evaluating each of the candidates, and not finding a single good thing to say. Most of them were cheerleaders. Cheerleading was currently number one on Abby's hate list since she'd failed to make the squad.

Write-ins were allowed, so the group would certainly find some other more regal candidate. That meant I would get shanghaied into making posters to support the upstart.

Walking into the crowded gym with Gabe hadn't been all that great. Many fingers had pointed at us. It was subtle and polite but pointing nonetheless.

Gilles van Nullens wildly waved to get our attention and scooched way over to make room for us on the bench.

After all the noise and nonsense was concluded, he walked to the half-moon with us.

"Sure you want to be seen with me?" Gabe asked us, more amused than bitter.

"Yah," Gilles insisted. "I know how it feels to be new. Many pupils teased my accent and mocked me."

"You?" I gasped, "Your English is perfect, and I know for a fact that not a single one of them can speak Belgian."

"Flemish," he corrected. "But yes, the crowd is like sheep. Any newcomer makes them nervous. But I promise it won't take long. For me, after a few days, I was —how do you say it? A way cool dude?"

I tried to laugh, but it wasn't the same at all. Gabe *had* been cool.

Yesterday.

After Gilles left, Gabe invited me to go home with him. And his dad.

"I called Mattie, and she said it was fine," he told me. "She won't send your sister after you."

"OK, I'd like that." And I meant it. The drive wasn't all that long, but maybe we could talk some things out. We walked to the limo, his shillelagh tapping beside him.

Still, I felt a lot of guilt that I hadn't done more to help him, that I had been so angry earlier. "I'm so sorry, Gabe. I don't know what set everybody off."

"I do. I'm somebody different. Maybe even a bit threatening."

"But you're not."

"You know that. They don't."

"Gabe, I didn't tell anyone the real reasons. I was tempted, but I'd promised. But you know…" I stopped for a second, but decided to try to convince him. "I think you ought to let me. I mean, you *are* recovering from a legitimate, very serious illness that isn't AIDS. You're not an addict and all that other crap."

He smiled. "I don't think the truth will matter. Remember what I told you the first day we met? I've been through this before. Suspicion. I guess even prejudice. I'll survive it. As long as you stay my friend." He looked at me once again in that half-lidded way, but I could still see sadness there.

"Oh, you don't even need to wonder about that." I promised, wondering if my heart was in my own eyes.

He was quiet for a while. "I hate to say it, Delli, but I think a lot of this has to do with your sweet little friend Abby. She's not going to go easy on me because of my dad. You know, him refusing to sell the property."

I was sure that was true, but I just couldn't keep the old loyalty from surfacing. "Gabe, I know she's got…problems, but I also know she's got a good heart."

"I hope so. But Delli, I'm going to say it again. Watch out yourself." He moved a little so he could put his arm around me, but it was more to reassure me than anything romantic.

But the circle girls are my friends.

I shook my head, both at Gabe's remark and to get the words out of it.

We didn't have much farther to go to get to Skyline Lane, but the car's smooth movement lulled me. After my miserable night, I closed my eyes. I knew Gabe wouldn't consider me rude or anything.

Even my legs felt thick and heavy.

15

She was so very, very tired. The walk from the village had taken so long. The swamp smells almost made her sick. What was it? Sulfur? Rotting flesh? Yet this was Gabriel's world. How could it be evil?

How could *he* be evil? He had been the victim of evil. Of folks needing a scapegoat to blame. Just like Salem.

Suddenly she saw him.

Without a word, he balanced his back against a large boulder and opened the circle of his arms. It seemed wherever he hid in the swamp, she easily found her way to him. She settled against him, and his long black cloak covered them both.

The softness of his long hair warmed her cheek. Sighing almost with contentment, she cuddled into him, like a child. Yet she felt herself a woman grown.

"I have missed you. But I knew you would be here today." His words were muffled against her prim white cap. Moving his hand from the folds of the cloak, he released their embrace while he pulled the cap from her head. The impropriety, the danger of baring her head alarmed her for a brief second. Then she relaxed. This was Gabriel. He would not mind her hell-fire hair.

But it was indecent to be so close to him. Was she damning herself no matter what? Yet wasn't the love of man and woman a blessing from the Most High? Indeed, Gabriel ran his fingers through her tight curls, his knuckles catching. But it was more pleasure than pain, licentious or not. For once, he was more real than mystery.

More good than lewd.

"How did you know?"

"The danger has built. I will protect you."

"How? Have you a weapon?" she asked him, her flesh prickling.

"I have my ways," he said without saying anything.

Protect me? Or lead me into temptation?

No. He had been raised in the church of his fathers.

Nonetheless, fright tripped up and down her spine in a nasty dance. Darkness pummeled her mind. Suspicion she couldn't control crawled over her bones. But Deliverance kept the words to herself. Last time she had seen him, she had vowed to stand by his side. But what did she know about this man? That he intrigued her? That in her shameful heart she wanted him to kiss her wrist again, mayhap her mouth?

How could she be certain that he wasn't a demon, as Abigail Williams and the circle girls claimed? She knew nothing of him but the words that his own tongue had uttered.

Gabriel...who may not be as he says.

What had put that uneasy thought in her head?

She fought for calm. *The Lord shall preserve thee from all evil: He shall preserve thy soul. The Lord shall preserve thy going out and thy coming in from this time forth, and even forevermore.*

She begged the beautiful psalm to become real. On her last visit, she had rejoiced that he had escaped discovery. He had disappeared into one of his lairs, and she had excused her traipse into the marshes as a search for mallow. The mob had believed her.

Or so she thought.

Ever since Goody Carrier's trial, the village had lived in a miasma of terror. The accusations went on and on. The girls called out name after name. And the Court condemned witch after witch. Not even the magic and strange medicine of the heathen tribes sharing this land had riled Salem Village so much.

The possibility of evil living in their own wooded marshes kept the good folk more on the edge of disaster than ever before. This panic and vigilance had forced Deliverance to remain close to home.

But today, she had chanced a secret visit. She eased back into the crook of his shoulder. This was Gabriel, named for an archangel. With his long hair veiling the ravaged half of his face, he looked as comely as any bachelor. Even with the unseemly length of his hair.

She understood why he kept himself hidden. Surely that hair was suspicious enough. But the rest of him, his gentle manners, his modest garments, surely these things would dispel any doubt that he was evil incarnate.

But what if he was? Her skin shivered along her bones.

What if the Highlanders had been right? She had only his word otherwise.

He turned to her as if with a kiss. Her cold unease burst into the heat of panic. She had changed her mind about wanting such a thing. About wanting him close. What if he was as people claimed? She moved from him, sad at her suspicions. He had spoken of God but had never in her presence recited the Lord's Prayer, which the demonic could only do backwards.

Dare she ask him to deliver the holy litany?

A shout split the dank gloom before sinking with an echo in front of them. Through the fog, she could see and hear the angry mob. Torches glinted off muskets and pitchforks and gleamed eerily through the mist.

"Here she is. With her demon lover. The daughter spawn of the witch Matilda Wyllys." The shouts hurt her ears. *The witch, Matilda Wyllys? Her honored mother had been arrested?*

Deliverance stood in horror as Goodman Abbot snatched her wrist in a cold iron grasp more a shackle than a human hand.

She turned for Gabriel, who had promised to protect her. Even as she had spurned him.

But he had vanished.

I will never leave thee, nor forsake three. The Lord's own promise from Hebrews. Deliverance sank to her knees. All she needed was God. She had no need for the trust of humankind.

~AΩ~

Fingers circled my wrist, and I tossed them off.

"Hey, wake up, sleepyhead. You're home."

Gabe's touch and voice were soft, but I reacted in horror.

A cold iron grasp more a shackle than a human hand.

"Sorry," I wanted to apologize more, but my voice shook. Even though I recognized instantly where I was, Deliverance's terror still lurked in my mind, my heart. Even though it wasn't me getting arrested in some fetid swamp that didn't even exist.

Mr. Wincott was pulling up my driveway. He was practically rubbing his hands together in glee. "Just let me know what you all want for this place, Delli," he laughed, trying to sound lighthearted. "I'd love to get my hands on 'er."

I figured he was probably making a joke, but I glanced at him suspiciously anyway. Abby's words from earlier that day echoed in my brain. "I can't imagine my dad selling. This is his heritage." I didn't want to sound snotty, but I did manage to keep my voice firm. We did need a ton of remodeling, though. I mean, a blind person could see that, but the house had lovely bones.

"Hey, just kidding around, Delli." Mr. Wincott smiled in a comforting way. "I already know that. We've met, and I like your dad. He's a good man to treasure his roots."

I decided to believe him. After all, I couldn't explain to either of them that I was upset for another reason. I grabbed my backpack and confessed a little bit, too. "I can't believe it, but I had a little bit of a nightmare just now."

"Crazy, A daymare? Man, you're shaking." Now Gabe's hand reached out to touch my hair or something, but I shook him away as nice as I could. I didn't want his knuckles to catch in my curls, like the swamp man's had.

My breath caught like the air was too cold. Of course I meant the way the swamp man's had caught in *Deliverance's* hair.

"Hey, what's up? Did I..."

I tried to laugh it off. This was Gabe, after all. "No, it's all me. I don't know, really. Mr. Gallindo's been talking about the Salem Witch Trials in class. For one thing, I can't believe Christian people treated each other like that. Plus, I've been thinking so much about what kind of project to do that I guess I've got, well, witches and weird stuff on the brain."

And you, Gabe. Gabriel. You who may not be as you say. I couldn't believe it, but my dream was making me look at him in a different way. The way the group at St. Bart's had this very day.

I hated myself. I'd promised to be his friend. Nothing about him was ravaged or suggested evil. His physical problems supposedly were pretty nearly healed. But what if Abby and all the rest were right? Maybe he really wasn't a mainstream, standup guy. I really didn't know much about him.

Except for his long hair and his pale face, he looked like most other guys at school. But I couldn't help remember how weird he'd been in the grove early this morning. Maybe he had been on something. And that stupid cape. Normal guys don't do stuff like that.

As sad as my suspicions made me, I couldn't stop them.

What if he was a stoner or addict of some kind? Maybe he did need the walking stick because he was weak from detox or rehab or something. I wasn't sure how any of that worked. My parents' wild youth and bad head trips had made them into extra-protective parents. Mattie and Chris had practically threatened death if any of us experimented with illegal substances.

One good thing. All their bad experiences and exposures to different dogma had led them to the one true God.

And speaking of parents, maybe his dad really was after my dad's property. What if Mr. Wincott *hadn't* been joking just now? What if Mr. Wincott was as greedy as Abby's dad?

I couldn't understand my funny feelings and I needed to escape. I moved to open the car door. Maybe it wasn't a leftover dream at all. Maybe Gabe himself was the reason for my feeling of doom. Maybe he was going to fall off the wagon and wanted to drag me down with him.

Maybe he was actually warning me about himself.

I didn't know what to believe. I had promised to be his friend, but like I say, I really didn't know him at all. At first, I had thought I wanted to know him and was glad to have what I thought was a cool neighbor my own age. But now I just couldn't be sure.

After all, I *did* know Abby, and Betsy, and Lesley and everybody else. We'd all been friends for years. Betsy and I had gone to the public middle school with Lesley until the Lebentals built a fancier house and sent her to the private one. And Abby had really protected me from gossip that first day freshmen year when I'd gotten dropped off at St. Bart's in my dad's crummy truck. It had stood out like a creepy prehistoric animal among all the sleek purebred Mustangs and Beemers.

Taking a deep breath, I turned to say good-bye to Gabe and to thank his dad for the ride. I could see that Gabe was disappointed because I hadn't gestured him to come along.

"Maybe I'll walk up to your place later or something," I said, not sure I meant it. "But I do have a ton of homework. I better get started. I haven't really decided about my project yet, and Mr. G. wants a progress check tomorrow."

"Well, OK. Get some rest. You look like you could use some."

I grunted a little. I wasn't very flattered hearing

that, but I hadn't slept well last night so I probably did look pretty decrepit. And I have to admit that I did regret the sad look in his eyes as his dad drove off.

~AΩ~

Nothing about the after-school snack Mattie made appealed to me, so I decided to get back into the journal I'd started in the midnight hour—the witching hour—last night when I couldn't sleep.

The journal of Deliverance's dreams, that is.

I had a gut feeling the content would rivet any reader, but I couldn't decide yet if I'd turn in my scribblings for my project. Mr. Gallindo would probably think I was taking drugs myself, or worse yet, was losing my mind.

That reminded me for an ugly second that maybe Gabe was losing his. He saw a shrink, and he had weird feelings. Maybe he was going to lose it and turn St. Bart's into a war zone.

The phone rang, and Betsy's loud screams totally brought me back to the normal chaos caused by Abby. I held the receiver away from my ear.

"Calm down, Betsy. If you don't *shut* up, I'm *hanging* up. You're hurting my ear!"

"Delli, Delli, can you come over here? Can you come help me?" Betsy was crying, but I could hear how frantic she was, too.

"Delli, Pixie's dead!"

I heard it all over again. Little Betty Parris. *There was a dog. The devil's disciple. It passed me in the street yester morn and gave me the evil eye.*

The poor creature of course had done no such thing. It was just an innocent victim of careless girls who had caused its undeserved fate.

Somehow, Pixie had met the same sad destiny.

Why hadn't I done something? Warned somebody? My stomach walls crunched together.

I felt like throwing up and swallowed a whole bunch of times before I could say anything. "What are you talking about? What happened? Where's Abby?"

"I don't know," Betsy wailed, "Remember, she said she'd feel stupid walking Pixie instead of a 'real' dog? So I went all goo-goo, thinking about poor Pixie being stuck with Abby all the time. Because I just know Abby won't play with her or anything."

Betsy stopped to gulp. She made a huge gurgling sound, and I almost felt the shaking sobs. I wished I was with her right now, to hold her, to say something useful.

Finally Betsy went on, "So I thought Pixie would have fun playing over here with Skippy and Bobo. Abs dropped her off here." Skippy and Bobo were Betsy's sweet Boston terrier and an even cuter mutt.

"Yeah, you did good. So?"

"Well, Mom was at the grocery store when Abs dropped me and Pixie off. Pixie was tucked all in her little carrier and everything. Then the three dogs were all playing really cute and all." She stopped to gulp and gurgle again. "But like usual, when Skip and Bo heard the garage door opening, they went flying through the pet door."

Betsy sobbed really hard now, way deep in her gullet. I was pretty sure what happened next. Why hadn't I warned Betsy?

This was my fault, too.

"Well, Pixie ran with them. My nails were wet so I couldn't grab her. Skip and Bo know just where to wait so Mom doesn't squish them...but Pixie...She *didn't* know. She *didn't* wait!" Betsy was retching now.

I felt cold, sick, and helpless. Why hadn't I warned Betsy? Even if no one else would or could understand my dreams, I should have warned Betsy somehow.

"Does Abby know?"

"No. She's out shopping."

"Well, maybe you should call her cell phone." I tried to sound stern, but my voice was cracking.

Betsy didn't say anything, so I tried again. "Bets, you're gonna have to call Abby. *I* don't know what else to tell you to do."

"You gotta help me, Delli. My mom's just bawling right now. You know her. She cries her eyes out just driving by the animal shelter. I called Dad at the fire station, but they're out on a response."

I murmured some syllables, not really knowing what words would work. I felt like bawling myself. Pixie was a cute little dog. Or had been at least. And I tried hard not to think of how messed up Mrs. Schemper was going to be about the whole thing. She was a lonely old rich childless widow, and Pixie had been her baby, her kids, grandkids and great-grandkids rolled into one little wiggly pup.

"Delli! What's Abby gonna say? Can't you come over here?"

"What's *Abby* going to say? How about Mrs. Schemper?" I realized I sounded pretty harsh, so I tried to offer more comfort. "Well, yeah, I can come over. And Betsy, Pixie's death was an accident. A terrible accident. It's terrible, but accidents do happen."

"But Pixie was my responsibility."

"No, Betsy. She was *Abby's* responsibility. Mrs. Schemper's paying her to take care of Pixie, and she obviously felt she had better things to do."

But as Betsy gulped helplessly, making very awful sounds, I understood the truth. Abby would make sure someone else took the blame.

And this time she would be right. Pixie's death was my fault.

16

I found my parents drinking herbal tea in the kitchen. If I didn't watch out, they'd make me drink some, too.

Too late.

"Delli, you look just awful." My mom's face crumpled. "Now come drink this. Peppermint. It'll settle you right down." She tipped the teapot into a hand-thrown cup. "I'm convinced you're coming down with something. You're just not yourself these days."

Well, I wasn't. There was a girl named Deliverance who snared herself inside my head. And other girls named Abigail and Betty and dead witches named Bridget Bishop and Martha Carrier who weren't really witches, and poor sweet dead dogs. None of this was the real me. I liked sunshine and the beach and pretty flowers. Classical music and good books. Soft kittens and tumbles of puppies. My mom's baby lambs.

No, none of this was the real me.

But for some reason, there was a girl in Salem whose skin I was living and sleeping in right now.

At least now I had a legitimate excuse to look and feel rotten. This time I didn't need to mention the dreams, or Salem, or wacky Gabe or any of that.

"Can somebody drop me off at Betsy's? It's a long story, but Mrs. Schemper's little dog just got hit by a car."

I couldn't mention that Betsy's mom had killed it

and the whole thing was my fault. That I could have prevented it.

My mom looked expectantly at me, and I shook my head. "Not now. I'll tell you later."

"Oh, my goodness, me." Mattie shook her head, "Ruth's heart will absolutely break without that dear little thing."

My eyes filled with tears. It wasn't just that Pixie had been a cute little dog with lots of years left. Mrs. Schemper was a nice old lady and a good customer at Mattie's shop. We loved her.

"I know. And it's my fault." Unable to stop the tears, I let them flow and threw myself into my mom's arms, just like a little kid. Sweetly concerned, Chris sat without a word, a bit confused as usual, stuck as he was in a house totally full of females.

"Honey, what do you mean?" he managed to ask. Mattie kept muttering, "No, no."

"Abby was watching Pixie and asked me to help her, and I blew her off." Not quite the truth, or all of it, but it would do for now.

"Now, don't you go saying any such thing," Mattie scolded in her practical way. "If Abby agreed to the task, it was her responsibility. Besides, you have plenty of animals around here to take care of."

That sounded logical but in reality I didn't do much for Mattie's sheep or chickens. Our wonderful Border collie Schatzi had died a year ago, and Chris didn't have the heart yet to replace her. She and I had been the same age.

Still, I couldn't shake the awful feeling that I could have warned Betsy somehow.

"Let's go in my truck." Chris drained his mug and stood up. "Your mom's car needs an alternator, and

Angie's off somewhere with the girls."

I dried my eyes and washed my face in the tiny powder room off the kitchen. Seeing my reflection only reminded me of Deliverance's face in the swamp pool. And the curls bouncing around my head only made her think of the swamp Gabriel and his fingers in my hair.

Well, in *Deliverance's* hair, I meant, feeling the prickles tickle my skin again. Would I ever get rid of her? Could I? Even if these were only make-believe dreams, I found myself wondering why he had vanished just when Deliverance had needed him most.

Unless he really was the Dark One, full of conjuring and black magic.

As I shook off the ugly possibility, Chris and I got into his battered old truck. At least we weren't driving over to Abby's ritzy neighborhood where the old rattletrap would make us look like servants. Betsy lives in a very nice neighborhood, but the folks there are pretty normal, like her parents. Firefighters and schoolteachers, optometrists and nurses. Unfortunately, Scat himself.

As we drove off, I glanced one last time at our house with a sinking feeling in my gut. Both Abby and Mr. Wincott were right. Even though it was still charming, the house needed some work. Not some, I reflected glumly. A lot. It wasn't even that my dad didn't want to spend the money. He and Mattie just didn't think earthly things needed much effort. As long as the roof didn't leak and the house stayed warm in the winter, their main concerns would always be keeping food on the table, growing organic fruit in the groves, helping at our church's soup kitchen, and stimulating inquiring minds at the bookshop.

Chris stayed quiet. He never said much anyway, and now he left me to my own problems. Just where Skyline Lane met the highway, my cell phone rang.

It was Abby, using a hissing sort of voice that might mean she was crying. "Hey you, just get on over to my house. There's a lot going on."

Well, so much for not looking like a green card servant. I sighed, still stinging with guilt. I owed Abby this much. Betsy, too.

"Yeah." Abby went on, "Betsy's over here. She needed to get away for a while. Mrs. Barich is carrying on so much."

Some of my sympathy for Abby evaporated. Abby actually sounded contemptuous, like Betsy's mom was weird. Maybe Abby held most mothers in low esteem after what had happened with her own.

Maybe I ought to warn Mattie to watch out. *The witch, Matilda Wyllys? Had Deliverance's honored mother really been arrested?*

I shivered as I hung up the phone. "Dad? Change of plans. Abby's house instead."

At Abby's private community, I gave my name to the keeper of the gatehouse, and he let us pass through without a word…And to his credit, without a wide-eyed sneer at our bashed-up truck. Abby must have called ahead to tell him she expected us.

"Need me?" Chris asked sweetly as I got out in front of the Goodmans' elegant house.

"Nah. But I'll call you when it's time to pick me up. OK?"

"All righty. And good luck. Love ya, honey." He leaned close to kiss me. Oh, I loved him.

Betsy was curled up in a sad little ball, trembling on the giant couch that curved around the *ginormous* living room. It had been specially made. Abby wore a brat look I was sad to recognize easily. Mr. Goodman broke into a huge sappy smile when he saw me, and he came over to gather me in a giant hug.

I had always liked Abby's dad. Well, until this Ms. Lipsett thing, that is. And him muscling Mr. Wincott to sell his land. Tom Goodman had never behaved snobby at all, even with his thousand dollar slacks and his perfectly cut hair that didn't even move in the wind. During Christmas break, he planned on taking us girls on a ski trip to Montana in his Learjet.

The trip sounded cool. And I hoped I'd be able to talk Chris and Mattie into letting me go. I had never been in a commercial plane, much less an executive jet. Getting my parents to agree was going to be a challenge, though. I could already hear their very words: "Such a trip is a blatant example of material excess and conspicuous consumption."

Well, they did love nature, and I'd never seen snow actually falling. So maybe I did stand an actual chance.

Anyway.

"I'm so, so sorry, sweetie." Mr. Goodman's words fell into my hair. "I'm sure Mrs. Schemper won't hold it against you. I'll help in any way I can. I'll contact her for you as we sort things out."

I pulled back from him, amazed. "What are you talking about?"

"I know my daughter asked you to help her out with that dear little dog, and you let her down." He shook his head sadly. "You must feel terrible. If only you'd been there…"

Even though I had felt my own sense of guilt, getting chastised by Mr. Goodman was something I didn't deserve at all. I wasn't sure I liked him anymore, ski trip or not.

I first gave Abby a dirty look then threw one at him. "I don't know what your daughter told you about today, but I didn't know anything about it. And of course, I feel bad. I love animals. But this was just an awful, awful accident."

I started to wonder just how bad Mr. Goodman had made Betsy's mom feel.

"I'm sure everything will be fine." He soothed but sounded fake, and for the first time, I realized I didn't know him—or his daughter—at all. "I'd like to let Ruth enjoy the rest of her vacation. Lord knows it might be her last one." He gave a sick little smile. "I think we'll just hold off on letting her know until she's back home. You and Betsy can explain it to her in person."

"Me and Betsy? What about Abby?" I also realized right then that I'd never be taking a flight in a Learjet. And I didn't care. "I don't know what's going on here, Mr. Goodman," I told him, using what I'd hoped was a very mature voice, "but Pixie was Abby's responsibility. Let your daughter do the face to face."

Then I shook my head at Mr. Goodman and gave Abby a dirty look after I turned to go. It would roll off her face like a summer breeze, but it made me feel better. I'd call Chris's cell phone as soon as I got outside. He probably wasn't more than a couple blocks away. I sort of hated to leave Betsy alone with them, so I offered her a ride, too.

Betsy shook her head, never moving from the couch. Ever the perfect host, Mr. Goodman politely walked me to the front door.

"You know, Delli, this hasn't been a very good day for you...us." He added the last word hastily. "Mrs.

Schemper is a reasonable person, but she is quite shortsighted where her little doggie is concerned. She has no other family, you know. I wouldn't be surprised if she…takes legal action."

His voice stopped dramatically, and I wondered just what awful thoughts—make that threats—he was getting ready to blackmail me with. Maybe he thought I owed him something just because he took me and Betsy with Abby to Disneyland every year, got us a fancy suite at a fancy hotel. And he'd always had his wife—well, ex-wife now—buy me totally designer stuff for my birthday. But things like that didn't mean he was a nice man. Maybe like a wild jungle animal, Mr. Goodman would do anything to protect his offspring.

I shrugged and dug in my pocket for my cellphone "Yeah," I said. "It's gonna hurt Mrs. Schemper a lot."

"You know, Delli," he continued smoothly. "I have an idea how many little struggles go on for your family. Your dad deserves a nice truck. You, deserve a classy set of wheels. A Camry. A Mustang. An A3 series like Abby's. You deserve to plan on going to the college of your choice and not have to worry about tuition.

"And…" He met my eyes and his had a strange sheen. "Then your mother would no longer have to try to make ends meet with her little pagan shop."

Pagan shop? What was he getting at? Was it he who had anonymously pointed fingers about Mattie's Aztec calendars? My breath froze in my lungs.

The daughter spawn of the witch Matilda Wyllys.

The crowd's ugly chant throbbed in my brain. All of a sudden, I knew where Mr. Goodman's thoughts were going, why the questions and guilt were being laid on *my* shoulders. The veiled threats against my mom. He wanted our home. These little suggestions—let's be honest, they were warnings—were supposed to get my dad to sell.

"I get it, Mr. Goodman. I know what you're implying right now. Somehow or other you're going to use any means at your disposal to get my dad to sell our place. Mr. Wincott wouldn't sell, but you're still determined to get your hand on Skyline Lane."

"Now, Delli. Sweetheart." Mr. Goodman used his businessman schmooze. "Chris is a reasonable man. He'd be a millionaire many times over."

"Money doesn't matter to him." I reminded this stranger I'd never known before. Chris truly believed it. "You know that."

"Money matters to everybody." He wrinkled his nose and still managed to look attractive. Rubbed my shoulder in a fatherly way until I shook it off. I knew better. As long as Chris kept us fed and clothed, he was content.

"Well then, go ahead and make him an honest deal." I shrugged. "Just don't get your nose out of joint when he refuses you. And don't try to mix up Pixie getting killed or my mom's eclectic tastes with more of your little blackmail or something."

His eyes narrowed. "What are you talking about?" Now he didn't look smooth, or even nice like he used to. Something about him was dark, shadowy. The Tom Goodman standing next to me wasn't recognizable at all. Suddenly I was sure my earlier instincts were correct.

"I mean, like you paid Ms. Lipsett back when she wouldn't go out with you. Maybe you suggested…something more than just a date even, and she just downright wouldn't have you."

I knew Mattie would be horrified, not only at my disrespect but also at the awful notions. Even if this pervert did think her a pagan. Yet I didn't take any of it back. I shut the door noisily and quickly walked down the long *cul-de-sac* to wait for my dad.

I didn't want to even breathe the same air as Tom Goodman. I wanted to get as far away as possible, and fast.

17

Chris could tell something was wrong as soon as I belted myself into the truck. As usual, he respected my mood after asking me if everything was OK. Well, it wasn't, but I gave him a generic, "Yah."

The Goodmans were insane. All of them. That was it. Now I knew why Mrs. Goodman had left. As we drove up Skyline Lane, I wondered how much of this I should tell Chris and Mattie. They tried to act all cool and blasé about conflicts and ruffles in their routines, but I had an idea they would be concerned if Tom Goodman was on the warpath.

When Chris parked his truck near the sheep pen, I noticed him. Gabe. He stood along the wooded lane with the last of the sunlight glazing his face, like the treetops had a hole in them. Just like on campus earlier.

Just like the swamp man had first appeared to Deliverance. My throat felt thick when I swallowed.

Gabe waved, but he looked kind of nervous, like I might send him away or something. Well, I was nervous, too, but I smiled and tried to be enthusiastic. We'd started off as friends. And after that uncomfortable ride home from school, I knew it was all up to me what happened next.

As he started toward me with his walking stick, Gabe looked more shaky than jaunty. Way more weak than hot. Maybe it was just the incline of the road.

I felt ashamed. I had liked him so much. Well, of

course I still did. But because he was different, I had let my mind go off an unpleasant track, just like the kids at St. Bart's had. Just like Gabe had told me people always did.

And I even knew the truth about him and his illness. What did that say about me?

Or did I really know the truth? Could God help me find it? After all, even Deliverance had some doubts about the swamp man's version of the Highlanders. Gabe had behaved so weird in the grove this morning. But at the same time I couldn't help think of the townsfolk in Salem, how sickness or strangeness got them marked as a witch. I needed to treat Gabe a lot better than that. He was my neighbor. I owed him a little loyalty.

Or in this case, a lot of it.

I got out of the truck and walked over to join him.

"Hey you," I called out, hoping I sounded cheerful. "You wanna sit for a while or walk some more?" I kind of didn't want to invite him inside in case Chris and Mattie were still in the kitchen. They were cool enough, but I knew that we wouldn't get any peace. But at the same time, I didn't want to go on a walk either. I really didn't want to wander around the grove. To remember that morning.

To be reminded of Deliverance in that awful swamp.

What had happened to the dream girl? Tomorrow was September 24. Maybe no court records existed listing Deliverance as a hanged witch, but why couldn't the frightened mob have taken matters into its own hands?

My skin crawled. Why had Gabriel abandoned Deliverance?

For that matter, why had I abandoned Gabe? Because I was afraid to stick up for him? I realized that my support and friendship would be huge.

"Hey, yourself," he called back, his jaunty self taking over. "I think I need the exercise." He grinned, somewhat hesitant, his face reddening. "Unless you're avoiding me, that is."

"Nah." I felt myself blushing as well, so I figured he knew I felt bad. Even still, I didn't know what to say. It would be nice to blow off steam about poor Pixie and Abby and nutso Mr. Goodman, but that would only strengthen Gabe's poor opinion of my friends.

Unless they really weren't my friends anymore. How could that be? Maybe…

A nasty possibility pulsed in my veins along with my heartbeat, a thought I just didn't want to think. What if, being a member of the board, Mr. Goodman had known I was about to enroll at St. Bart's two years ago and ordered his daughter to be nice to me? To get to my dad?

Gabe's grin faded and brought me back to reality. "I creeped you out this morning, lurking in the grove," he muttered. "I'm so sorry about that. I had no right to trespass."

"Bull. My dad said you could take a walk over here any time you wanted." I assured him. That was true. But I avoided replying to his first statement. It *had* creeped me out, big time. You know, my going down there and him saying he had known I would come.

Then I asked myself why I didn't just tell him? Weird things were happening to me, too. He was just having feelings. I was actually having dreams that seemed to come *true*.

Well, not true exactly. But they seemed to have counterparts in the here and now.

"Well, yeah, a little creeped out. I gotta confess. About the grove, I mean." I relaxed, trying to smile. "But I've been feeling pretty freaky myself. You know, those bad dreams about Salem and all."

"Wanna talk about it?" His voice and eyes were kind. Why not? Besides, close up he didn't look shaky and weak any more. And he smelled great, woodsy and oceany all at the same time.

"OK. Why not? I guess so. Maybe." I babbled like the idiot I'd been at eleven.

We started walking down Skyline Lane. It is a lovely country road that snakes up and down a hill. For once, my feet felt light, not like they were stuck in muck. Or nightmares. He was standing close, his stick on the other side, like a shepherd's staff. I was sure he could hear my sigh of relief.

I had no reason to be self-conscious any more. Gabe had confided in me once, after all. So I started to talk.

"It's just....well, some of the dreams take me to a swamp where I...run into this mysterious man. Our grove isn't at all like a swamp, of course, but it is dark and leafy and then twice now, you've been there. Sort of like the dreams."

"Well, should I be flattered that you sort of think of me as a mysterious man?" Gabe tried to chuckle. I thought he might be trying to be a little flirty, but his eyes had sort of a worried tweak around the edges.

I giggled like that eleven-year-old I'd been; just wishing we both could relax. The wind started heating up, and that tends to make folks more antsy than ever. "I know it sounds all crazy, Gabe. I just...well, I just usually don't have such vivid dreams. These sort of tell a story. And sometimes, well, you're going to think me a whack job. Sometimes Mr. Gallindo in American Lit will teach us something that I kind of already knew from the dreams."

"Dude." That was all he said, but I knew he was thinking hard about what I said and didn't think I was wacko. Then he was quiet for a while, like he was considering something. The gravel atop the asphalt road crunched beneath both our soles and the stick.

Soon we came to Mr. and Mrs. Jumper's big charming home, old like ours but well-maintained. For a horrible second, I wondered if Mr. Goodman was panting after this place, too.

Just thinking of the awful man reminded me of Pixie. I told Gabe about the little dog, and what was going on with Betsy and Abby. And about my own part in it, too.

My guilt. My fault that Pixie was dead.

"You can't possibly believe you had anything to do with that poor dog getting run over, do you?" Gabe's fists tightened around the stick.

I didn't reply right away because I could hear Betty Parris shouting, *There was a dog. The devil's disciple. It passed me and gave me the evil eye...* Of course, I had something to do with it.

Because I'd done nothing at all.

Just like Deliverance, who should have taken the Salem dog home and made it a pet.

"Well, do you?" Gabe's insistence brought me back to now. "I already told you that Abby is selfish and sneaky. If she can push this off on you and Betsy, she will. Don't let her."

"But..." I knew all of that, but I couldn't help

revealing a little of the situation. "Mr. Gallindo was telling us about an innocent dog getting hanged as a witch, and I felt so awful. Then to have this happen the same day."

"Animals are always innocent," Gabe said. "When God told Adam to subdue the earth, He didn't mean torture and exploit them."

This sounded way too much like Mattie. Even though I agreed, I still ate meat. So I fought to find another subject. The only other one of any importance in my life, for now at least, was the unbelievably believable dreams.

"I know. It's just that...Pixie and that poor dog hanged in Salem make me feel sick."

"Hey, don't beat yourself up over any of it." For a brief, lovely second, Gabe stopped and touched my cheek. I felt happy that I didn't want to brush his hand away. Then he spoke thoughtfully. "You know, Delli, I think our subconscious holds a lot more than we think. I mean, maybe you saw that movie *The Crucible?* Or maybe you paged through your textbook when you were bored one day and didn't realize until now that things were sticking in your mind."

I realized he was not speaking just to comfort me but to tell me what was probably happening. He did make a lot of sense. I nodded.

"You could be right," I admitted. "I've never been to Salem, so I can't even imagine if the area even looks like the place in my dreams. I mean, of course the town and village would have changed over three hundred years, but I mean, the terrain. The geography. Have you ever been there? Do you think there's a swamp or a marsh outside the town?"

Gabe shrugged. He was walking pretty steady

now, resting his stick on top his shoulder like a baseball bat. Now that he was well balanced, I began to wonder if he would reach for my hand.

I wondered if I would let him, or if I would shake him off like a fly. The touch on my cheek had been nice.

He answered my questions instead. "I haven't been there either, but I know the area's coastal. I guess there could have been marshes or swamps back then. Maybe they got drained over the years." For a second, he pumped his stick like a drum major's baton then rested it on his shoulder again. "The only swamp I remember from American Lit came from the most amazing story by Washington Irving, 'The Devil and Tom Walker.' Have you guys read it yet? There's a neat picture in the textbook that goes along with the story. My dad used the same book to home-school me last year."

I shook my head. "We read stuff in chronological order so Mr. G. can tie in the history, too. We're not really doing fiction yet. Puritans now, Revolutionary War stuff next."

"Well, it's a great story about this guy, Tom Walker, who takes a shortcut through a swamp. Tom runs into a weird, dark stranger who just cut down a tree." Mature trees lined both sides of the road. Gabe stopped in the shade to lean against a fence. I stood as close as I could. He ought to narrate audio books. His voice was great.

"The tree had a rich man's name carved on it," Gabe said. "When Tom gets home, he realizes that a rich neighbor, Absalom Crowninshield, just died. The stranger was the devil who took back the soul Crowninshield traded to him during life, so

Crowninshield would have earthly riches.

"So you probably saw the picture of that swamp paging through the book or something."

Maybe. Possibly. Probably. *Certainly.* Of course! Because that was a name I remembered from the first dream. Goodman Crowninshield.

The name from a nightmare.

But even with the audio book voice, more nightmarish was hearing Gabe speak of a dark stranger that people sold their souls to. I clearly remembered Deliverance wondering if the mysterious stranger was the Dark One.

Then I threw off the ugly thoughts and feelings. I wasn't in a dark swamp, and Gabe wasn't a mysterious stranger. He was my neighbor, my friend, and God was my refuge and strength against Satan. The bright afternoon in late September was very warm, with a dry, hot breeze. Just like normal.

My breathing came easier for the first time in days.

Certainly just now, Gabe had given me an intelligent reaction to my problems. Now more than ever he deserved to have me help him with his own.

"I don't know what happened today, Gabe. I've pretty much always liked the kids at St. Bart's, but there's a pretty wealthy segment who might be threatened by you." We started walking again. "I mean, you're amazing looking with a hint of mystery. Your dad drives a Rolls Royce and obviously has celebrity connections. That's all a threat to their cool status quo." I looked closely at him, and he nodded a little like I made some sense.

Then I went on. "Of course there are a lot of normal kids there, too. Like Betsy and me. We don't pose much of a dilemma, especially if we hang out with the right group.

"In fact…" My voice slowed as I recalled the first time I'd met Abby, how Chris had delivered me to campus in his old truck, and Abby hadn't minded a bit. So I told Gabe the truth. "Abby hooking up with Betsy and me so early freshmen year probably eased any sort of question about us being acceptable."

I didn't mention my horrible doubts that Abby was using me. But I sighed over the sound of our shoes scraping gravel. Everything would be so much nicer if everybody in my life would just get along. Besides, I was pretty nice to know in my own right.

Gabe shrugged. "I guess she might mess with me because my dad bought the property her dad wants."

I didn't say anything. He might be right. Even if Abby hadn't made up the rumors, she had admitted to spreading them. But I wouldn't put it past her dad to start something. Tom Goodman seemed intent on doing and getting whatever he wanted, and he was head of the school board to boot.

Maybe tomorrow would be a better day for everybody. Even if it was September 24. I shivered a little in spite of the hot wind. Maybe I needed Gabe by my side as much as he needed me. "I sure hope you're gonna go back to school tomorrow."

His smile was wry, crooked as we rounded a curve. "Yeah. It takes a lot more than a rumor to knock down a Wincott."

We both laughed. With him having stared death in the face, St. Bart's snotty little gossips were probably a piece of cake. Plus he'd indicated that he'd braved gossip before, that God had helped him through worse times than this. Just past the Jumpers' circular driveway, he started to turn around, and I followed without comment. It hadn't been much of a stroll for me, but after all, he still had to make it to the top of our lane, and he might be feeling overexerted. My heart jumped when he put his hand on my shoulder and clasped it.

"I'll be there tomorrow. Right by your side," I promised. If Deliverance had done more of that—sticking up for those she knew were perfectly innocent instead of running scared, maybe more of her neighbors would have escaped the gallows.

As I finished speaking, Gabe lowered his arm to take my hand. His fingers felt wonderful, warm and soft, even with the guitar calluses. Long fingers that could make music.

La-a-a. La-a. La. La. La-a. La. La. La-a. La-a-a.

For some reason, the notes playing in my head didn't scare me this time. I seemed to have won that strange skirmish.

"I'd invite you to dinner," I said happily, boldly, "but I better find out what we're having first. My mom doesn't fix any kind of normal food. Nothing with eyes, of course, and she either grows or imports everything else. She's got some old hippie friend who is now a totally organic farmer in Guatemala or somewhere."

"And you?"

"I adore animals, but it's true, I have no trouble scarfing down cheeseburgers." I laughed. Cheeseburgers were normal. So every day. And I needed a dose of normal about now.

"Well, this weekend I'll take you out for one. I think I'll pass on Guatemalan imports for now. No offense," Gabe said, his eyes opening and his teeth grating like I really might be insulted.

"No offense taken." I gave him a farewell squeeze of my own at the screen door. No big deal, but my heart was light. This was pretty much a date, in my book.

As I watched him walk away, I liked what I saw, what I knew. I was certain that the student body at St. Bart's would, too, in no time at all. Then I nearly screamed in disappointment when Angie announced that she'd be calling in a pizza delivery. Chris and Mattie were going off somewhere, so we had to take advantage of the situation.

I realized I could call Gabe and ask him to come back over for pizza, but somehow, going out alone with him on the weekend would be worth the wait. Plus, we might remind Angie of how much she missed Glen. Maybe I wouldn't even mention the date.

"He's cute," Angie told me with a smile, but I could see the sadness there and was glad of my decision. She and Glen had been high school sweethearts. Angie held a cup to her lips. "Want some tea? Actual Earl Grey. None of Mattie's mixtures, I promise."

I don't know why I agreed, it being a warm late afternoon and all, but all of a sudden, tea sounded good. She poured me a cup.

"How do you suppose we ended up normal?" I giggled, dumping in three giant spoonfuls of sugar.

"I'd say luck, but I think it's totally Chris. Dad, I guess I should say. He managed to change with the times and let us be who we wanted to be." Angie laughed back. "I think Mattie would be content to still live in a commune somewhere, calling herself Blooming Iris. And remember, we're just two of five. The other three..." Angie's eyebrows raised high up her forehead, and we both groaned with affection. They'd all found their ways. Our brother Will worked at a mission school in Uganda that he'd help found and was translating Bible stories in Tooro for the kids. The identical twins Peony and Patience, one a hospice nurse, the other a doula, spoke together in their own private language. They had a written alphabet for it, too. And these were activities Mattie encouraged.

Knowing that, I wondered for just one last time whether or not I should confide in my mother. But things seemed logical now. Gabe had explained them pretty well.

So my sister and I chatted for a while, just like sisters everywhere. Then I excused myself to start my homework. Writing in Deliverance's journal was a must, and I had plenty of time before dinner to knock off a bunch of pages. I just might chance it and turn the whole schmear in for my American Lit project.

Now that Gabe had told me some logical reasons for my dreams, I felt more relaxed than I had all week. I let the peace of the Lord settle on me. Until something else came to the front of my thoughts. Mattie and her methods of feeding her family. Her rye flour scones. Mr. Gallindo had said something about rye flour getting contaminated and making the folks in Salem have visions. Maybe something like that had happened to all the staples Mattie imported or grew and stored herself?

Something that made me dream. Made sense to me, so I put the warm cup to my lips.

18

She drank gratefully from the steaming pewter tankard, holding it as well as she could since her hands were bound with rope.

Governor Phipps had forbidden the miserable chains, but the mob, having witnessed Deliverance in the arms of a preternatural being, had demanded strict measures. Her honored mother's hands were hot as they tried to embrace her on this chilly September eve.

For some reason, Sheriff Corwin managed daily to slip them some costly treats. Neither Deliverance nor her mother had any idea of who might be willing to assist them.

Her honored mother whispered, low, although the other prisoners mewling about the cell gave little notice. The straw-covered floor was dank and foul. Many of the accused were busy with their own sickly children.

"I wonder how your sister Patience fares with my kin in Marblehead." Matilda's hands reached out to stroke the matted hair of little Dorcas Good, whose mother had swung from the gallows weeks ago. Aged four, Dorcas was an accused witch herself, but one of the few in jail who warmed up to Deliverance. Perhaps because she was too young to understand the particular nature of Deliverance's crime.

"It is indeed kind Providence that you could secret her from Salem before...before this," Deliverance whispered, more worried about her mother than a healthy young sister safe with kin.

Her mother's face was pale, her skin hot, her voice raspy, as though a plague ravaged her. Deliverance was not surprised her mother had taken ill from the malignant humors and foul air of the cells.

Her honored mother had told her about the bachelor from Andover who desired their farm. After Matilda's gentle refusal of his marriage proposal, it hadn't taken a day before accusations flew.

"But Deliverance, why will you not speak to me of your whereabouts on that fateful day?" Matilda managed weakly. "I could not leave without *you*. For you to be accused of—consorting with the Tall Man himself..."

Deliverance said nothing. That way her mother could never be compelled to speak of things she did not know. Goodman Giles Corey had been crushed to death just days ago, refusing to speak testimony that would make his farm forfeit to his family. Yet his goodwife and seven others would die tomorrow. Selfishly, Deliverance thanked God that she and her honored mother were not scheduled for execution.

Not yet at least. She raised her tied hands to her mother's face, hating the searing heat of the flesh beneath her fingers.

Many here in jail planned to gain release by confessing to mild versions of the false transgressions charged to them. But Deliverance's own misdeed was particularly horrible and likely not redeemable. She had been seen, and by many. Abigail Putnam and Anne Putnam, once her friends, had claimed to the court that *they* had seen her commit the sin of concupiscence with this very same demon. Perhaps the prince of the air himself.

It was all a lie, but Deliverance had been seen in the arms of a mysterious man. Who would believe that he was not evil incarnate? After all, she was the daughter of Matilda Wyllys, most certainly a witch.

You see, Goodwife Wyllys's full food stores and healthy gardens were proof of her conspiring with the devil. He could make crops wither and die—as had happened throughout most of the countryside to those who opposed him. Just as he made crops flourish for those who worshiped him.

Deliverance sighed in hopelessness. The court would keep her imprisoned long enough to see whether or not she was breeding an imp or demon. Of course she wasn't, but it would buy her some time. After all, John Procter had swung from the gallows, but his pregnant wife Elizabeth was spared for the time being.

True, Deliverance had never even touched her lips to Gabriel's, but shamefully, she had longed for his company. Aye, she must bear guilt for such longings.

Her shameful searches for him in the marshes that had led her and her mother to their doom. Had she remained at home, behaving like a proper careful daughter, she could have escaped with her young sister, and their mother, too. But no, because of her selfish pursuits, her mother had been unable to find her when the time to leave had come.

Deliverance sighed, and each drop of blood coursing her veins shuddered throughout her body. She knew that Gabriel was not a demon. He was not the devil luring her to her damnation. While he certainly had not delivered her from evil, she would keep her heart from hardening. She would.

He had promised to keep her safe. She had to believe him. Surely God had sent him as the instrument of her release.

Her heart hammered at the newest urgency afoot. In just moments, her examination would begin. The examination for witch's marks. When goodwives would strip her garments from her and prick her with pins.

In a panic, she checked. The half-kiss upon her wrist had long faded, but this examination could indeed bring death. Deliverance's body was gently peppered with raised freckles, marks believed to suckle demons. The good folk of Salem would eagerly believe them as proof. This was far worse evidence than little Patience's innocent husk poppets that had been construed as witch dolls.

Her honored mother's lovely face had aged ten years in these horrific days both with worry and illness. Deliverance's clammy fingers tried to cool Matilda's terrified face.

"How I would that I could spare you this indignity." Her mother sobbed. "But dearest one, you must be brave. In case my weakness does not allow me to live."

The keys rattled in the barred door of the cell. In their weary terror, many of the other prisoners scarcely noticed. Righteous and important, a gaggle of goodwives began their plod across the crowded floor.

"Mother, do not speak so." Deliverance whispered, pained. "You have an ague. That is all. I will somehow persuade Sheriff Corwin for some nourishing broth and some willow bark. Some feverfew."

The last herb only reminded her of the day she

had met Gabriel in the marsh. Goodman Crowninshield had always seemed a good friend.

She asked her mother straight out. "Would he be of help?"

Matilda shrugged impatiently, whispering so softly that only Deliverance could hear. "I know nothing of who remains our friend. Absalom Crowninshield, Sheriff Corwin. Mayhap. Mayhap not. All I trust is the Lord. His will be done. If this injustice brings us to His side in heaven, well, it is His will. But it may not be our time. Either way, you must know of my plans to grease the palms of the jailer. I think he can be bought with a heavy purse of gold. But I have yet to hear from my brother."

Deliverance was both excited and terrified by this announcement. Human greed had permitted Philip English and his wife to escape to New York. No doubt a purse of gold could work one more time. They could be reunited with precious Patience. But she would never see Gabriel again.

She knew in her heart he hadn't abandoned her. Circumstances might seem otherwise, but she knew it. Somehow God would direct him to save her.

Save them.

But instead of Gabriel's warm hands, the fingers on her were cold. The goodwives touched her everywhere, but they were not the tender fingers of a gentle husband. These were invaders, cold and frightening.

And Deliverance gasped in fresh terror with each shriek of triumph, each new freckle and mole that served as proof of her cohesion with the devil. She groaned as a needle passed, painfully, through one little mound of flesh. Ah, the pain disproved a witch's teat, but oh, there were so many others. She kept her eyes shut, her skin hot with humiliation.

Somehow, God would save her, and He'd use Gabriel to do so. It just wasn't going to happen now.

~AΩ~

I opened my eyes, afraid and not knowing why. My room was dark and very hot. Gracey and McKenna were playfully dragging my hairbrush across my arm. My skin prickled. I'd spilled the tea all over my bed, and my little nieces shrieked with glee.

"G'amma's going to be mad at you!" Gracey chanted.

Grandma! Mattie! Remembering the dream almost knocked my toenails off. It had to be a warning that something was going to happen to my *own* mother. I ignored both the tea mess and the little girls.

"Come on." Gracey pulled on my hand. "Mommy got us a pizza. She says for you to come eat."

I nodded as I sprang from the bed. My heart raced a million miles an hour. The tea had spilled across the pages of Deliverance's diary, but I knew the hot dread of the last dream would remain fresh in my mind for a long time.

A long, *long* time. I didn't need to hurry and scribble it down just now. Was Mattie in danger?

Oh, from the Proverbs. *Her children arise up and call her blessed.* Dearest Father, bless and protect my honored mother.

If Mattie was in danger, how on earth could I explain? Then I calmed down, remembering Gabe's kind, logical explanations. Mr. Goodman's mean-spirited remarks about Mattie's "pagan little bookshop" had inspired this dream. And I was still feeling the guilt of abandoning Gabe today. That was enough to make me dream that I really was guilty about something.

And that my mom was in danger.

The smell of pizza wafted upstairs, and at that moment, I felt hungry. But I saw the huge baked circle in the middle of the kitchen table, and I turned away. It was slathered in swirls of red sauce.

God will give you blood to drink.

The tea in my tummy sloshed around in an icky way. At least there was a green salad, with no tomatoes in it. I knew I better eat something, or Angie would tell our mom. Then I'd get dosed yet again with Mattie's personal versions of modern medicine.

"Hi. Help yourself." Angie switched off the nightly news. I had heard enough on the way down the stairs to know that Angie wouldn't be in a good mood. Reports from the Middle East these days were never very pleasant. So many service people were deploying home, but not Glen, not yet. "Oh, Abby called a while ago, but I told her you were napping. She left a message that she's sorry about everything. She was 'way wrong.'"

That sounded a little encouraging, and I figured I might be able to handle some pizza after all. At least the pepperoni, cheese, and dough part. "She say I should call her back?" I asked hoping she hadn't.

In spite of Abby's apology, I really didn't want to talk to her right now. I was still mad at Mr. Goodman, so I was glad when Angie told me *no.* "She said she'd see you tomorrow."

"Where'd Mom and Dad go?" I asked, more for something to say than really needing to know.

"Tom Somebody is taking them out for dinner to make them—and I am quoting Dad—an offer they can't refuse. Dad laughed when they left, said he was expecting a horse's head in his bed tomorrow morning." Angie shrugged. The family has seen *The Godfather* a bejillion times.

I shook my head so Angie didn't see, and I didn't say anything to her. Obviously, Tom Goodman hadn't given up. But my sister's worries about her soldier husband were far more serious than any of this.

My parents were grownups with strong wills. They'd never cave, no matter how hard Mr. Goodman worked on them about driving cool cars and sending me to a fancy college and having a million bucks in the bank. Chris and Mattie could always be counted on to retain their principles.

But still, I couldn't keep my skin from crawling. I'd never had lice, but I figured this must be how they felt. In my head I kept hearing Mr. Goodman remarking about my mother's pagan little bookshop.

And I could still hear Matilda Wyllys's feverish, raspy words.

You must be brave. In case my weakness does not allow me to live.

~AΩ~

I figured I should find Gabe. After all, he'd confided in me about his feeling of doom. He probably wouldn't think I was all that weird. Besides, there didn't seem to be anybody else to talk to. I'd need to warn Mattie, but she wasn't home. I wasn't going to fail this time.

"I'm going for a walk over to Gabe's," I told

Angie, not asking permission.

"You didn't eat much dinner. Don't you have any homework? Besides, it's dark."

I didn't pay any attention. "We don't exactly live in a high crime area," I reminded her. "Besides, it's not far, and I won't be long."

Gabe was chatting with his dad at a patio table. Mr. Wincott was smoking a cigar, something Mattie heartily preached against, but I saw Chris sneak one once in a while with Hank our foreman.

Mr. Wincott greeted me, grabbed some dirty dishes, then left us alone.

Gabe smiled in a glowy way that made me believe he really was glad to see me.

"Want some dinner? Dad's a great cook." He grinned, and knowing he was thinking of Mattie, I laughed out loud.

"I mean it," he chuckled.

"Nah. We actually had normal pizza tonight." I didn't mention I had barely been able to swallow any, much less the reason why. "My folks went out. That's why I'm here. Mr. Goodman invited them to dinner."

I decided to wait a minute to share my feelings that Mattie was in danger, sort of ease into the subject first.

"That's nice." Gabe shrugged. I could tell from his careless gesture that he still wasn't much impressed with Abby and her dad.

"No, it isn't, Gabe. I know he's going to start in on wanting to buy our property."

My voice must have risen in a scary way, because he instantly took my hand and spoke in a soothing manner. "Delli, it's going to be fine. Don't worry. Even if he does offer, your dad will say no. Besides, when I mentioned this to my dad, he said Mr. Goodman was very reasonable, very polite, when Dad declined his offers."

"Well, you know Abby. I..." I couldn't help it. My fingers tightened around Gabe's hand, and I looked him straight in the eyes with all the honesty I could gather. "Listen, Gabe. I'm afraid. I think something bad is going to happen to my mom. Mr. Goodman said something today, in a rude way, about her 'little pagan shop'. The place is eclectic. Egalitarian."

"That's a mighty big word." His grin melted my heart.

"Vocabulary assignment." I punched his arm lightly. "What I mean is, if you don't like her stock, don't buy it or read it. Don't come to the shop. But what if..." Terror funneled like a tornado in my head. "What if she and my dad say no, and he starts to sully her reputation? Like she's a witch or something. Or a pothead. You know. She could lose her business."

He bent his head, his smile and words kind. "You know, they say even bad publicity is good publicity."

I was so angry I tried to pull my hand away but he held fast. Why had I thought to confide in this goon? And what if Mattie didn't take me seriously either? I know she and Chris trusted God with their whole hearts, and I was supposed to, too. But...I might as well finish what I'd started. "You don't understand, Gabe. It's...well, tomorrow is September 24."

Shaking his head, he agreed. "You're right. I don't get it. What's tomorrow?"

Then I broke down and told him everything. The dream-Deliverance now in prison, ready to be hanged. Her honored mother dying and maligned. All because someone wanted the Wyllys farm.

I even mentioned again the poor hanged dog in Salem, and what had happened to Pixie. How Abby had blamed me and Betsy. How I'd even blamed myself.

And Mr. Goodman's unconditional support of his daughter no matter what she did.

Just like the parents in Salem.

But I didn't mention anything about swamp-Gabriel. I just couldn't. That is, nothing other than what I'd told Gabe earlier when we were discussing the mysterious man in the swamp. That would serve no purpose, mentioning how Deliverance had been abandoned when she needed the swamp man most.

"Hey." Gabe was almost stern now but his fingers were gentle. "Some parents never admit their kids do anything bad or wrong. Don't sweat it. That's really sad about Pixie, though. I'm all for owning up when you make a mistake. But Delli, tomorrow is just a day like any other day. Honest." He looked away, almost a little embarrassed. "After I talked to Dr. Stan this morning, I knew what had caused my fears: nerves about starting at a new school." He picked up a tall glass and sipped from a straw. At least he wasn't drinking tomato juice.

"Maybe that isn't a trauma like...like losing my mom," he went on, "but it still put a lot of anxiety on me. You know, after all the stressful things that have happened to me lately. Dad and I don't have a church in town yet, so I called our pastor back home, and he prayed with me. I know I can face anything. And you, don't worry. Your mom's going to be fine. She's a professional businesswoman, and from what you've told me, she's no naïve kid. She's a woman of faith, and she's been around. Plus you said that Abby had apologized."

He put his finger under my chin, gently, not romantic at all. He was just comforting me like his kind nature would comfort anybody. We still had our cheeseburger date coming up, and that was probably just a friend thing anyway. Then I remembered something.

"But you said your feelings of doom were about...*me*. That *I* was in danger."

"Yeah. Dr. Stan explained that I might be sublimating. Big word. Means that I was so scared about myself that I was too embarrassed to admit it. You were on my mind a lot." He gave me a shy little smile which made my tummy tumble down a few inches. Maybe it was a real date after all. "So I made *you* out to be the one who would need help. That way I could be all he-man and protective, not a wussy baby off to his first day of school." His cheeks grew a little pink.

That all seemed to make sense. Most of what Gabe had said recently did.

"Well, OK. That's good then." In a real fit of daring, I leaned over and kissed his cheek. Gently, not romantically. At least he had revealed that I wasn't in any sort of danger. I might as well relax. "Gabe, thanks. Thanks for listening to me. You helped a lot. Honest. About why I might have those dreams, and well, just some of my own anxieties. I want God to fix things now. Right now, you know? Patience is so not one of my virtues."

Then I saw the headlights starting up the hill. "I better go. That's probably my parents. I can learn what's going on, if anything. Anyway, it will be interesting to find out what my mom ordered to eat."

We both laughed.

In spite of the afternoon's hot winds, the evening had turned dewy and chilly. Looked like the devil winds had spent their three days in town and gone off until next time. I must have looked bright and healthy for once because my mom and dad didn't stop laughing with Angie when I walked into the kitchen. Lately they'd been annoying and attentive, watching me like a hawk. Peering at me like I was going to collapse any second or something.

"Wassup?" I asked, glad that they didn't look all panicked or anything.

"We had a lovely evening with Tom at the Tower Club," Mattie said. "Even though he made no secret that he's quite interested in the place. And willing to pay a pretty penny." She winked at my dad.

I'm not surprised, I thought. Aloud, I had to ask. "Well, you're not going to sell, are you?" I had to admit, thinking about a cool car and going to college was fun, but it would never be enough to change my mind about my heritage.

"Absolutely not," Chris announced. "But I didn't refuse him right then. I told him I'd have to think about it overnight. Talk it over with your mom. And pray about it without ceasing. I'll get back to Tom tomorrow."

"He probably thinks you're playing hard to get and will up the ante," Angie decided. "Better watch out for that horse's head after you count sheep tonight."

"No," Chris laughed, "that would be *tomorrow* night."

We were all laughing, but the horse's head reminded me that none of it was funny. I had a feeling

I'd seen the real Tom Goodman earlier that afternoon.

"Has he ever offered on the place before?" I asked, suddenly interested.

"Yeah. A couple of times, but not for several years."

Hmm. I chewed my lip. Maybe that *was* the real reason Abby befriended me that first day at St. Bart's. In spite of my dad's awful truck.

19

Across Gallows Hill, the sea wind whipped her skirts topsy-turvy. Deliverance could hear the horrified murmurs as the billowing fabric bared her ankles, for such was grave immodesty.

She stood on a chair, the rope taut around her neck. Already her throat was stifled. For an insane second, she wanted to laugh. The gathered crowd cared more about her indecency than her death.

Nearby, her honored mother sat on a hard chair, stiff and pale. Too weak to walk, she had been carried from jail so she could watch the punishment. Matilda Wyllys was too ill to stand, too close to death herself to warrant execution. The bachelor, Inigo Abbot, had even offered to marry the widow Wyllys in spite of her crimes before she succumbed. But Deliverance knew the real reason. He wanted the farm.

Witnessing her daughter's execution, the court had determined, would be penalty enough for Matilda Wyllys. Deliverance's monthly courses had come. She did not bear the demon's seed. She was ripe for execution.

Over the droning wind, the reverend recited Scripture. The crowd moaned. Deliverance felt both terror and hope. Gabriel had promised to save her. He had promised. God had provided.

Provided her a mansion in heaven. Throat heavy, she could not sound out the Our Father, significant proof of her innocence.

Inside her head, she prayed. *Into thy hands I commend my spirit.*

A strong gust blew the first of fall's leaves from a branch, and through the twigs, Deliverance could see him. Could see the edges of his cloak furl and unfurl like the sails of a black galleon.

Could see his hair both hide and reveal the ravages of his own punishment.

He had come.

She could not point; her hands were tied. But something in her gaze, her demeanor, deflected the crowd's attention to his direction.

He stepped closer. The frantic gathering gasped as one.

"She is no more a witch than you are wizards," Gabriel announced loudly, pointing a long elegant finger at the reverend, then at Judge Noyes and Judge Hathorne. "Cut her down."

"It is him. The Dark One," shrieked the circle of girls who had helped bring the nightmare down on Salem. "It is the one who consorted with her in the marshes."

"The Tall Man!" howled Goodwife Ann Putnam.

"Cut her down," Gabriel ordered again.

"I say we obey him," cried Reverend Samuel Parris to the judges, he who was himself terrified by the croaking of spade-footed frogs. To see an actual ghostly figure must be playing true havoc with his mind. "We have no choice."

"To cut her down is to succumb to the power of evil." Judge Hathorne shook his noble head. "We are placed in this city on the hill to resist the powers of darkness."

"Nay, Mr. Hathorne. I, too, say let this girl go," wearily announced another magistrate, Judge Sewall. "Perhaps we have resisted evil too forcefully. Twenty of our friends and neighbors now lie in unholy graves. Whoever this dark stranger is, let him take her from us. Then we will be rid of them both. Let her go."

"Aye," Gabriel said again, "and I shall take her mother, too. Let the greedy bachelor have their land. In the oncoming years, watch carefully how little it will prosper him. It came at too heavy a price—the cost of his soul."

"Let her go! Let her go!"

With one voice, the crowd began to shout for Deliverance's release, just as wildly as they had once screamed out accusations.

~ΑΩ~

I woke up in peace, my heart beating fast but peacefully. Gabriel had saved Deliverance, and her honored mother, too.

He hadn't abandoned her.

It was September 24, but I knew now that I had nothing to fear. Relief calmed me. Deliverance had not met her fate on this date, three hundred years ago. Gabriel had protected her just as he'd promised.

I breathed easier than I had in days and might as well ask Mattie for some tomato juice for breakfast.

That would be the real truth serum.

Mattie didn't have any, though, and deep inside I was glad. Better not rush things. Gabe called, laughing that "the limo" would be by to take me to school in a half hour.

Greeting Gabe like a long lost friend, Abby and

Betsy met us at the half moon in front of Swink Hall. Betsy still seemed a little shaken, but Abby looked completely contrite. I knew Abby well; her repentance was genuine.

We all hugged and did the air-kiss thing. Even Gabe.

"Sorry about Pixie," he offered in his nice, kind way.

"Yeah, thanks," Betsy replied, cheeks pale, hair dull. "But my mom's still way freaked."

Abby blushed a bit, taking Betsy's hand and looking at Delli.

"We all are. Daddy was able to reach Mrs. Schemper ship to shore or something. Actually, she was very understanding and decided to finish the cruise. Just like Daddy said she should. Daddy promised to meet her at the port in a limo with a new puppy. And have Pixie taxidermied or something"

Yuck. But I didn't say the word out loud. If Mrs. Schemper was very understanding, she wouldn't be taking legal action or anything. Of course, that could have just been Mr. Goodman blowing smoke to make me and my family feel threatened.

But why not let bygones be bygones? I had never been much of a grudge holder.

"You know, why don't you two come spend the night?" I invited, meaning it. "Give your mom, Bets, and your dad, Abs, a little peace? Maybe I can help Angie cook something normal for dinner, and Gabe will want to come over, too?"

Everybody nodded, and I felt a sudden surge of affection for my friends. We'd just hit a rough patch yesterday. Everything was OK now.

Until we got to the quad where everybody

congregated to wait for the homeroom bell. Everywhere were posters publicizing the candidates for homecoming queen. But someone had maliciously decided to promote a new candidate.

Signs emblazoned with "Gabe Wincott for Queen" were everywhere. Of course, the signs didn't have faculty approval; someone must have sneaked on campus during the night.

Another low blow, just because the guy was new and different. I turned to glare at Abby, but Abby was way too upset.

"I had nothing to do with this, Delli. Gabe," she announced through gritted teeth, running all around, tearing down the offending signs. Making a huge production while she did it.

Looking distressed, Gilles van Nullens joined her.

Then Gabe did the best thing he could. He grabbed a brown lunch bag from a trashcan and quickly fashioned something. A crown. He put it on his head and went to stand by a sign before Abby got to it. In front of a whole mob of kids, he pointed to the offending words, strutting like a supermodel on a runway, and laughed out loud. Just like he found the whole thing funny.

Sweeping low to the ground in a melodramatic Musketeer way, Gilles bowed to Gabe, himself shaking with amusement.

Soon the student body of St. Bart's was laughing, too.

~AΩ~

It probably was one of the best days of Gabe's life, I decided. He had shown his confidence, his power. By the end of the day, he was the popular, hot, new guy once again.

And after his bow, Gilles had whispered to me, eyes sparkling. "I think now I will spare myself the rejection of asking you to the homecoming dance."

I laughed back. "No one has asked me, as a matter of fact."

"Yah, but he will."

After that, my day had turned to normal, too. Abby was best friends again after the militant campaign of removing the awful posters and championing her new friend, Gabe. Even American Lit had gone back to being nothing but another snoozer class. We'd finished with the witch trial stuff and were learning about some other Puritan who lived later on, a preacher named Jonathan Edwards. He totally ranted and raved about how God wanted to hang sinners over hellfire like a spider on a web.

Those Puritans sure didn't seem to enjoy much.

Mr. Gallindo explained that Jonathan Edwards was the start of something called the Great Awakening, a time when Puritans and everybody else relied on knowledge instead of superstition and finally got it through their heads how dumb the Salem stuff had been.

I was interested for about a nanosecond when Mr. Gallindo mentioned a little postscript about Salem one more time. *None of the circle girls had ever gotten punished for the tragedies they had instigated.* And only one, Ann Putnam, had ever apologized, fourteen years later when she was all grown up.

Well, at least Abby Goodman knew when to apologize.

And Judge Nicholas Noyes, whom Sarah Good

had cursed with the God-will-give-you-blood-to drink thing, had actually died choking on his own blood after some sort of seizure.

"Sarah, you go girl!" Josh Taggart called out, and I felt a sort of justice for those people Deliverance had known so long ago.

~AΩ~

Just before dinner—Angie had decided on pot roast for everybody else and a stuffed eggplant for Mattie—Chris came in from the groves.

"Hi, Delli. Gabe." Warily he glanced at Abby and Betsy, but must have realized that the clique had normalized. "Betsy. Abs."

The girls waved back, and Gabe got up to shake his hand. We'd been snacking on a huge wedge of Mattie's sheep cheese, and some crackers she made herself from cracked wheat. They were shaped like shamrocks, and I decided that meant good luck.

For the first time, I considered how truly amazing my mom is. She works full time, runs her own store, and yet manages to keep alive many of the home arts of generations ago.

A strong woman like Matilda Wyllys, who had managed to hold together her household and farm during the ravages of the witch hunts. I really hoped Deliverance's mother had gotten well from the ague— whatever that was—that had nearly claimed her life in jail.

If she had even been real, that is.

"Sorry, man," Chris was saying to Gabe, pulling his hand away. "I'm pretty grubby. Forgot my hands need a good scrub. In fact, the whole bod does. I'm gonna go upstairs and *ablute*."

"Ablute?" Abby and Betsy both asked at the same time.

"Bathe." I laughed. Chris was trying to be funny, and for once, he actually was. Maybe because for once, there was another male present.

"Hey, Dad," Angie called from the kitchen where she was teaching McKenna and Gracey how to rip up lettuce. "Tom Goodman left a couple phone messages."

"Yeah, I got him on my cell."

"Well, not that it'll be any big surprise, but what did you decide?" I asked my dad.

"Mattie and I both decided," Chris declared, "and you're right. No surprise. We'll never sell."

First he gave Abby a little apologetic smile then did a thumbs-up to Gabe and me.

Abby had tensed. I couldn't miss the signs, but she seemed to relax right away. By the time she left the room, muttering something about misplacing her purse, I'd pretty much lost interest. Gabe was sitting next to me, after all. And the cheese was actually pretty good.

All around me, I heard the friendly chatter of Gabe and Betsy. Above my head, I heard the rumble of water in the old tub upstairs.

And suddenly, I heard Abby scream like the devil himself was after her.

20

"He...flashed me, Daddy. He exposed *it*. It's called indecent exposure," Abby sobbed, not daring to look at me. "And you can't believe what he said he wanted to...to do to me. The old pervert."

My skin threatened to crawl off my bones. My dad looked like he'd died a few days ago.

"I'm going to call the cops," Tom Goodman yelled, louder, bigger, and meaner than I could have imagined. The kitchen was normally such a peaceful, fragrant place. He practically blocked the whole old fridge Aunt Jeanette had left. Suddenly I understood how scary it was to mess with him.

"I was taking a bath." My dad wasn't as tall as Tom Goodman, but he was darn well holding his own. Everybody else sat rigidly at the kitchen table, but my dad had refused to back down. "I told the kids that when I went upstairs."

"I just needed to pee, Daddy," Abby said smoothly. "The bathroom door came right open."

"The lock in the door is old and doesn't catch right away. Even my little granddaughters know to knock just in case. I'm sure Abby knows that, too. She's been here many times." Chris faced Tom Goodman, resolute then pointed. "And she darn well knows we have a powder room over there."

"He was...naked, Daddy." Abby covered her face with her hands. I positively saw her smirk between her fingers.

"I was taking a bath!" Chris thundered. *"You* intruded on *my* personal space, young lady."

"Don't you dare yell at my daughter." Tom Goodman spoke through slit lips. "Abby, tell me the truth, darling. Was Chris merely taking a bath?"

She moved her hands and peeked. Oh, yes, I knew that smile. It tolled a death knell for my dad. Tom Goodman would never believe that his darling daughter was lying.

"Yes, he was, Daddy. I admit that. But when he saw me he...well." She looked away from her father, blushing prettily. "When he saw me...he, well, winked at me and grabbed *it* and waggled *it* at me. If you know what I mean. Then he said he wanted to, you know. That horrible word. He said he wanted to do it to me ever since he met me. Then he stood up...Oh Daddy." She buried herself against her father's chest.

Chris had paled whiter than death, and I witnessed my first taste of adult reality. Tom Goodman would believe his daughter sight unseen, no questions. He was just one of those parents. And he had the resources and legal contacts to bring down my dad. Chris was in a great deal of trouble. I knew it, and my heart almost exploded. Child protective services always erred on the part of the minor child and might even remove me and my nieces from our home. And just sorting out my dad's innocence would cost him a fortune in legal fees.

Money he didn't have. Unless he sold our home.

I gulped but nothing happened. My throat felt all clogged up, like the drain when the garbage disposal didn't work. Like Deliverance's had with the rope taut around it. All this time my dad had been the one in danger and all this time I'd thought it would be Mattie.

Just as I thought of my mom, Mattie came home from work. She was singing one of her own songs as she opened the kitchen door. Mattie smiled at Tom Goodman until Angie pulled her aside with a whisper. Then our mom roared to life like a jungle creature wanting to rid her habitat of a dangerous serpent.

"I think it best you leave our home, Mr. Goodman." Mattie faced off Tom Goodman, using the voice that sent shoplifters running for their lives. "My husband did not expose himself to your daughter. Nor suggest rape. The child is making mischief because my husband refuses to sell to you. For shame. To think we had a lovely time with you last night."

Well, Mattie's tone usually worked even on non-shoplifters like her husband and her children, but Tom Goodman didn't move. His eyes didn't even blink. Abby snuggled against his side like she was cold.

"Come on, Annabel." Tom's lips were stiff. "Betsy?"

Betsy Barich followed Abby like always.

"Willis, I'm not done with you yet," Tom Goodman announced in a cold dead voice so different from his bellows.

~AΩ~

I felt like an ice sculpture, cold and unable to move. Even in front of my parents and big sister, Gabe had taken my hand, but even that didn't warm or animate me.

He stood up and as soon as he loosened my fingers, I felt empty and colder yet. "Listen, I'd better go." His manners were superb. He hesitated a polite second before adding, "Mr. Willis, my dad knows some good lawyers. He's had some Hollywood buddies who got into major trouble. That's why he's always been so strict with me." His lips tightened in a grim little smile that normally I would have thought adorable.

If my world wasn't coming to an end.

"Yes, Gabe, thank you. I'll touch base with your dad if I need anything. Anyone."

"Pick you up in the morning?" Gabe asked me before he headed to the kitchen door. In our shock, none of us Willises remembered our manners enough to see him out.

I shook my head. I was never again going to set foot in that snake pit. What would the St. Bart's clientele do with this latest gossip if a new student merely getting driven to school by his dad could cause such chaos?

My dad was getting accused of indecent exposure, for heaven's sake. By the daughter of a big-time contributor who was on the school board. By the time school started, Abby would probably have exaggerated her lie to include attempted rape.

"Bye, now," Gabe said, giving me one last look that let me know he'd be there for me whatever it took. At least that made me feel a little bit better. He mouthed. *I will be with him in trouble; I will deliver him.* And I knew the verse from Psalm 91 right off. Gabe had mentioned it on the way to school.

Then Mattie spoke from the dinette chair where she'd collapsed. "You know, I've had a few moments to settle down. Maybe this isn't Tom's doing at all. He's just protecting his child. I'm sure it's Abby just up to mischief. Likely she's feeling her dad is beaten because we didn't take him up on his offer."

Chris nodded, but I knew better. I'd heard Tom pointedly remarking about Mattie's "pagan little shop."

"I wouldn't put anything past either of them," I insisted, my voice sounding as frosty as my body felt. I was shivering like I'd been asleep without covers. "I'll bet Abby's only been my friend all these years, so her dad could get his hands on our place." I looked at them to see if my words were sinking in. My parents actually listened.

"He was probably just biding his time because he wanted the Lynch property more, but now that it's off the market." I finished.

"Well, I think I better talk to Mike Wincott in the morning about an attorney," my dad said as he got up to lock the kitchen door. "And I thought I was such a cool dad when I walked in and saw you kids having a good time."

"You were, Chris. You are." I threw myself into his arms, hoping that using his first name made him feel a little bit better.

"My darling." Mattie went even farther as she drew him close. "You know I'll be by your side no matter what."

"You always have been," Chris said into Mattie's long gray hair. "And we've got God there, too. We're going to beat this thing."

Mattie was so calm, so upright, so confident—just like Deliverance's mother in spite of her ague. I didn't mention it though. My parents had enough on their minds without contending with a daughter who was either psychic or wacko. Instead, I grabbed the edges of the kitchen chair I was sitting on like I needed to keep from sinking. I begged for a replay of Gabe's parting verse.

I will deliver him. Her. Us. Me.

Then Angie spoiled everything, trying to be all reasonable. "Well, maybe we should look at this for a minute from Abby's point of view. I mean, all the girl does is go up to pee and opens an unlocked door. Here's a totally naked man in the bathtub who was just scrubbing his privates or something. I mean, maybe she's never even seen a naked guy before."

"Yeah, right," I scoffed before warning, "But don't even go there, Angie. Mr. Goodman may not know what Abby's is doing, but *she* knows. I know. And you know our dad never had those thoughts or said those words. Come on, sis. Grow a brain."

21

I didn't have any dreams that night because I didn't sleep at all.

By dawn, my head ached from tears, lack of sleep, and more anxieties than even Dr. Stan would know what to do with. I'd prayed, grabbed my Bible, and reviewed the passages I'd highlighted to get myself through other horrible times, and discovered a hundred more. But I still felt like a wreck.

Why couldn't it be a weekend? I'd have church tomorrow to help clear my head besides not having any reason to think about St. Bart's anyway. But it wasn't Saturday. No way could I face two hundred pampered kids who believed my dad was a pervert. Chris and Mattie wouldn't make me go to school today, would they? Under these circumstances. No way.

Well, I was wrong.

"You're going to school. Willises don't go into hiding," Chris announced over a cup of coffee. Angie had insisted on brewing a pot of the real caffeinated stuff, not Mattie's preference of something boiled from chicory.

Both my lips and stomach twisted. I'd been trying to brave a bowl of flax bran. It was just how I envisioned the scraps inside Chris's secondhand paper shredder would taste if I added milk.

At least Mattie let us drink regular milk from dairy

cows, even with hormones and all the rest of the conditions she deemed inhumane. She'd long ago realized keeping a cow on the property just wouldn't work. Her sheep were enough.

"Dad." I didn't quite know whether to use that, or Chris or White Sage. Although I never use the latter. It was such a private thing between him and my mom. But today was so, so odd. Maybe it would help.

Well, whatever name my dad was going by today, maybe he was right. I ought to go down fighting, to do my best to silence Abby Goodman.

To stick up for those I cared about. Unlike what the people of Salem had done.

A friend loves at all times!

Gabe was on the same page, too, and Mike Wincott was absolutely militant. He managed to drive us safely to school, while using the speaker on his car phone to yammer angrily at some attorney.

Although I was seriously tempted to key the paintjob of Abby's precious 3-series Beemer, I resisted, even managed to keep my cool in the parking lot. To match my mood, the morning was damp and gray, more swamp weather than the Santa Ana winds.

"What do you think you're doing to my dad? To me?" I could hardly grind out the words as Abby climbed out of her car. I kept my fingers nailed to my thighs just in case. "I thought we were friends."

"I saw what I saw." Abby's nose rose way up in the air. "Daddy's calling the police this morning."

At first, I was too amazed to find words. Then they came in a torrent. "You're a liar. An idiot. A faithless… tramp. You've known my dad for years. He's a man of honor who loves kids. Who would never do anything to hurt anyone. In any way. And you know it."

Abby didn't reply at all, busy as she loaded her backpack with makeup, her cellphone, laptop and a designer makeup case. Her Biology text and a notebook lay forgotten on a pile of cashmere sweaters on the front seat.

"I'm talking to you, girl." I grabbed the shoulder strap of Abby's backpack. "You better lay off my dad or I'll..."

"You'll what?" Abby demanded sweetly, slipping from the strap to let the backpack fall nonchalantly to the ground, "Turn to your mom who practices witchcraft?"

"Witchcraft?" I had to laugh at the absurd notion. "She's a practicing *Methodist*. You've gone to church with her. Gone to the Lord's table with her."

"Pish tush," Abby quoted from a Mary Poppins movie or something. "What about her labyrinth? Her crystals and hemp products in her store." Then she picked up her backpack and swished away.

I wanted to scream. The labyrinth like at the cathedral at Chartres? The gemstones that shone in other craftsmen's handmade jewelry?

What was wrong about those? Abby was Salem incarnate. But mixed in my anger was fear. I had nowhere to go but my knees.

And I did it right then and there, in the parking lot. In front of her and anybody else around. God wasn't going to forsake me.

Even still, I wanted Gabe at my side, but he was a senior with a different level of classes. I had to brave my classes by myself and probably wouldn't see him until the nutrition break. I sort of hated the reality of needing someone at the moment, but hey, what were friends for? To my total delight, I never worried even for a second. The Lord had been with me all the while.

Josh Taggart came to the forefront right away, loudly defending my dad. "That Abby. What a brat. Mr. Willis is one cool dude. He helped me tame a wave at the Rincon. And Delli's mom. She mixed up some *arnicus* or something to get me through football last season when I sprained a ligament. I never felt any pain at all. They're on it, man. That Abby...she's whacked, man."

And that's the sort of thing I heard all day long. How my cool dad had made a ton of guacamole for last year's homecoming barbeque and cooked pancakes all day long at the alumni breakfast. How my mom's homemade candles had made over five hundred dollars for the yearbook. How my folks both judged the speech marathon every year.

Nobody at all believed Abby's rants. Everybody said they liked seeing me at prayer.

By 3:00 PM, I'd had seen the best of humankind. The snake pit had buried itself. Deliverance might have lived in Salem, but I didn't. In my world, folks supported each other. They didn't point fingers. And if someone else did, they learned the truth first.

But the best came at the end of the day. When I waited for Mr. Wincott at the half moon, Gabe told me. "I just told everybody, I was like this weird dude in a cape who walked around an avocado grove uninvited. And this cool old dude told me to 'make yourself at home.' And I didn't even know he had a beautiful daughter at the time. You."

I turned hot and cold at the same time. Beautiful? Nobody had ever called me that before, other than Chris of course, and he had to.

~AΩ~

Even still, the police came to question Chris about seven o'clock that evening. Unbelievable.

My parents had behaved in an amazingly relaxed manner since I got home from school. Apparently, my dad and Gabe's had done a lot of strategizing all day and made some consultations. In fact, an attorney was visiting at this very moment. Maybe they all knew something I didn't.

Whatever was going on, McKenna and Gracey knew something important was up, because they were more obnoxious than usual. I had always figured I wanted kids someday, but after a month with these two, now I wasn't so sure.

Gabe had come for dinner, not even caring what might be on Mattie's menu. He had assured me a whole bunch of times that he knew my dad was going to be completely exonerated. I asked him for details, but he said he'd tell me later.

What was going on? He wasn't going to tell lies, was he? I'd begged forgiveness for all of mine.

"Don't bother, officers." Gabe walked over to the arresting officers, speaking in a manly way that countered no disbelief. Maybe I ought to trust him like Deliverance had the swamp man. "I've already told Mr. Willis and his counsel that I am prepared to sign a sworn affidavit." Gabe was confident, standing tall.

"You see," he went on never looking at me, "I overheard Annabel Goodman tell her friend Betsy Barich that she would bring down Chris Willis in any way possible because of a property dispute."

When I heard his words, I gasped. How was this possible? I didn't make any kind of scene, though, and, took my cue from my parents. They were as laid back as usual. I figured they already knew what Gabe was up to. But why had Gabe kept such a thing from me?

When on earth had he been around Abby and Betsy anyway to listen in on their gossip?

Then I turned cold all over. What if it wasn't true? Would he lie for me, put his own integrity in danger? After all, Deliverance's Gabriel had endangered his own life by facing the angry suspicious crowds.

"What are you talking about?" I whispered, trying to keep the doubt out of my voice. "When on earth were you ever around the two of them? Except yesterday, that is, and I was with you the whole time?"

"Wait a second." He went over to the attorney and excused himself after a few moments and nodded politely at the officers.

"Let's go outside," he said to me.

"OK, but Gabe, what's going on? What's all this about?"

He took my hand as we went outside and down to the grove, among the deep dark trees where it had all begun for me and I realized, for Deliverance, too. But he remained silent just a second too long, and doubt turned me to ice again. I had to let him know my feelings about this. He couldn't lie, not for Chris. Not for me.

"Gabe, listen, don't do this. I mean, don't tell a …I mean, don't make something up. It won't help anything. My dad will get through this all on his own. He's an honest man."

Through the trees, some moonlight flickered and landed on Gabe's black hair like snowflakes in movies.

"I'm not lying, Delli. I'd never do anything like that. Not even for you." He tossed me a crooked and breathtaking smile. "But I have to be careful how I word things until I talk to Betsy."

"What do you mean?"

He took a deep breath. "I know she'll cave. She's not very strong, and I think in her heart, she's a good person. Like I told the attorney just now, I need a little time to get the evidence that he needs."

"So you *are* just guessing!" My mouth opened big, my chin to my neck. What horrible game was he playing? This was my dad, my home. Although I agreed totally with his assessment of Betsy, it was a huge leap of faith that he could get Abby's little clone to think one thought for herself.

Or worse, get Betsy to admit Abby did or said anything wrong.

I looked away and tried to find something to stare at besides trees. I just couldn't bear to learn the truth about his dangerous plan. What if his leap plopped him on his face? It could be the end of my dad, my home. Our reputation, our way of life. "So what you really mean is, you're just *hoping* that Abby said something like that."

"No. I *know* she said it, Delli. There's no guessing. It's not just an idle hope. I just…" He stared off into to trees himself. "I just don't exactly know where and when."

"What? You heard her but don't know where and when?" All those rumors about how weird Gabe was smacked at my brain. He heard the incriminating words but didn't know here and when? Was he hallucinating?

"Just what are you talking about?" I accused, then took his face in my hands so he had to look at me. "What are you trying to pull here, Gabe?"

"Nothing that you can't understand, Delli. You best of all. You see…" His voice slowed down. "I heard them. *In a dream*. Last night. I was hiding behind some tree branches, wrapped in a black cape, my feet stuck in muddy muck. They were dressed all old-fashioned, in dark long dresses. But they were one and the same."

I shivered like it was winter. I knew I'd been in that same place, wrapped in a drab cape, muck sucking at my feet. But how had Gabe? More than that, why?

"But why didn't you tell me? Why did you wait until now?" I was both hurt and angry. Our avocado grove had sure become a place of wild emotions. But shocked as I was, not for a second did I doubt the validity of his dream. Not after the week I'd had.

He took a deep breath. "I needed to find out what other people thought about my, well, my premonition." He looked away. "You already thought I was pretty much a nutball."

"I did not!"

"Aw, come on. Admit it." He pursed his lips tightly in another funny but amazing smile.

"Well, OK. But I did change my mind enough to tell you about the dreams of my own." I couldn't help but feel angry. "Well, who'd you talk to? Dr. Stan? Your dad? Your pastor?"

"Yeah. All of them. But I mostly wanted to talk to your mom." Looking away from me again, he fought for words. "I can't explain it. I just had an instinct she would understand."

For a second, I really regretted that I hadn't done the same with Mattie, trusted her, confided in her. Maybe a lot of this could have turned out differently if I'd just let someone else into my head. Like I'd let Gabe into my heart.

That night, I stayed up way past the witching hour to finish my project, *The Diary of Deliverance Wyllys*.

Things were going to work out for my dad. I knew it. We weren't going to be surprised. God had promised never to leave us or forsake us.

But what did surprise me about that night was my falling on my knees and praying for Abby.

~AΩ~

It didn't take much at all to get Betsy to tell the truth to the police. She did have kindness in her heart, which is the reason I'd liked her from the start.

Gabe didn't even have to confess his premonition or whatever it had been. I figured we'd be good friends and neighbors for a longtime. Maybe more than that when the time was right. After all, we'd both had gone places we'd never really been and met people who had helped us.

People who may or may not have been real.

As for Abby....well. Not unlike Ann Putnam and her friends in Salem, three centuries ago, she managed to maintain her position at St. Bart's. Maybe someday she would apologize, but I was pretty sure that would take a lot longer than fourteen years. Ms. Lipsett acted quickly though, filing harassment suits against both Anthony Scatabello and Thomas Goodman.

The next Monday, Mr. Gallindo asked me to stop by his desk after class. He had found the original of that newsletter project while tossing out some old papers. A former student had made it a long time ago, in 1981. A year that meant nothing in the grand scheme. Mr. Gallindo made us date all our assignments, and it was dated September 24. Maybe that meant something. Or not.

The name Deliverance Wyllys didn't appear anywhere.

I couldn't help a sigh of relief even though I knew Deliverance hadn't really been hanged. She hadn't been real.

Still, I knew I hadn't imagined seeing the name on the photocopy. I'd think about that some other time. Talk to my mom about it.

"Now, young lady, as for your own project." Mr. Gallindo brought me totally back to now. He sounded kind of stern. Was he giving me an F? I was on scholarship, after all. Mattie and Chris had determined that I'd finish up at the snake pit.

Worried, I looked at Mr. Gallindo.

But his eyes were bright. "It absolutely riveted me. I stayed up until two o'clock this morning finishing it. Where on earth did you get your ideas? I felt like I was right there!" He smiled with real respect.

I smiled back and answered him the only way I could. "Yeah, Mr. Gallindo. I know the feeling."

Epilogue

Duntroon, Scotland
Late August 1696

The Grampian Mountains bowed their heads over a blue-gray tarn. Gabriel held his wife's hand tightly as they crossed the stepping stones of an icy burn, careful not to wet their feet.

Deliverance had survived New England winters in a drafty saltbox, but she had never been cold through the bones like here in the Highlands. The small, burned-out stone castle given them by the laird was a tunnel of wind needing a thousand repairs.

But it was home. And the Lord in His providence had brought them here.

Atop the hill, she could see smoke rising from the decrepit keep's chimneys. Ah, her honored mother was bound to have a hot broth waiting.

Indeed, God had gathered Matilda's strength inside her to survive the long ocean crossing four years before. However, small Patience had remained in the Bay Colony with her kinfolk, there better to school herself and wed properly when the timing was right. Before they set sail, Governor Phipps had released the horde of "witches."

"Shall we see how your fair maither fares?" Gabriel smiled at the drift of smoke. A brisk gust of cold wind lifted his hair from his damaged face. The sight no longer terrified the humble crofter families who lived in these spare parts. Deliverance had instantly taken to their kind, innocent ways and knew she had finally come home. She worshipped in their kirk and had learned to help birth their babes.

"I canna understand it, leastways explain it." Gabriel's face lowered to hers with a whisper as though he had a dreadful secret to impart. She raised her ear to his lips, liking his soft breath, liking the burr in his voice that had come to new birth since his return to his native land. "But the dreams come more and more often these days."

"Well, love, you best keep them to yourself." Deliverance warned, anxiously looking around as though the mountains and lake had ears. "Lest you bring darkness upon your head once again."

"Aye, but to you, my heart, I can speak of anything." He slowed his pace a bit as though to linger on the words. "The lass is like you, but her eyes are as green as the tors, and the lad limps a bit. Yet while I feel their young friendship is wholesome and pure, I canna divest my sleep of a feeling of darkness. Of danger."

He turned to Deliverance worriedly.

She touched his cheek comfortingly. "Nay, rest your anxious thoughts, Gabriel. Trust in the Lord. You are but an angel of light. 'Tis but a dream."

"I say my prayers. But night after night? With wind more hot and dry than skin can bear. And trees that bear strange green fruits. I do not recognize these things. What think you it means, wife?" She tried to laugh in spite of the lice-crawl of anxiety that crept up her spine. Were they not safe even yet? "It means that you have a bright imagination, husband! And what a blessing God has wrought. It should lend itself well should you compose a ballad of faeries and sprites that you could sing with your flute!"

As she gave him a playful push, she yanked gently on his long hair. "Mayhap at bedtime you need a stronger drought of that 'liquid gold' so dear to a lad's heart," she teased.

But Gabriel didn't even so much as smile. "You dinna think I've got the sight? I remember a time or two as a child. Once I dreamed of a three-petaled flower, and my maither's ewe birthed a lamb with three heads..."

"Nonsense," Deliverance scolded, suddenly panicked. "The future is the Lord's alone. Should you see the future, you would have prevented your...calamity. And my own. Now, let's not speak of these things. They are but dreams."

The sun broke through the low dark sky like the clouds had a hole cut in them. The glaze of unexpected sunlight touched Gabriel's face like a blessing.

Like it had the first time, she had been led to him in the swamp.

"Aye, wife, I think you are right, after all." Gabriel turned his face upward to smile at the brief warmth. "Just dreams."

Hands clasped, Gabriel and Deliverance walked up the hill. Then letting go, he dug through his pockets for his little flute.

"Aye, my flute. Let's march to song," he told her as the clouds covered the sun once again.

La-a-a. La-a. La. La. La-a. La. La. La-a. La-a-a.

Author's Note

Although I've used actual people and dates in my 1692 world, *The Circle Girls* is a work of fiction. This story is meant as an example of people's reluctance to respect the differences of others. People often cast blame and bully those who are not quite like they are.

The advice we are to take from the Gospels (Matthew 7:12; Luke 6:31) is simple: treat others the same way we want to be treated—with respect.

If you are the unique-but-different victim, or one who doesn't have the confidence—or the friendships Gabe has in the story—to resist bullying and taunts, please don't suffer in silence. Talk to your parents, a favorite teacher, minister, a trusted neighbor; look for anti-bullying support on the Internet—find the comfort and aid to help you cope.

I hope the message in *The Circle Girls* will help us each to remember that in the sight of God, every one of us is fearfully and wonderfully made. (Psalm 139:14). We've been created in the image of God, and He doesn't make junk!

S.D.G.,
~Anya Novikov

Thank you for purchasing this Watershed Books title.
For other inspirational stories, please visit our on-line
bookstore at www.pelicanbookgroup.com.

For questions or more information, contact us at
customer@pelicanbookgroup.com.

Watershed Books
an imprint of Pelican Ventures Book Group
www.PelicanBookGroup.com

May God's glory shine through
this inspirational work of fiction.

AMDG

www.ingramcontent.com/pod-product-compliance
Lightning Source LLC
Chambersburg PA
CBHW020613180626
46810CB00007B/2754